SURRENDER TO THE SHEIKH

THE SHEIKHS OF HAVILAH
BOOK FOUR

DIANA FRASER

Surrender to the Sheikh
by Diana Fraser

© 2021 Diana Fraser
dianafraser.com

Playboy sheikh Xander wants a trophy wife, while fiery sheikha Elaheh has no desire to marry—but when duty forces them to work together, their mutual dislike ignites into something far more dangerous. As tensions rise and sparks fly, a threat to Elaheh's safety forces her into Xander's protection. Can their growing attraction bridge the divide between them, or will it push their countries toward conflict?

—The Sheikhs of Havilah—
The Sheikh's Secret Baby
Bought by the Sheikh
The Sheikh's Forbidden Lover
Surrender to the Sheikh
Taken for the Sheikh's Harem

—Desert Kings—
Wanted: A Wife for the Sheikh
The Sheikh's Bargain Bride
The Sheikh's Lost Lover
Awakened by the Sheikh
Claimed by the Sheikh
Wanted: A Baby by the Sheikh

PROLOGUE

Shakira, Queen of Jazira, adjusted the cushions at the small of her back and eased back onto the chair, her hands cupping her pregnant stomach. She gave an exasperated sigh and looked at each of the three original kings of Havilah—Amir, Zavian and Roshan, her husband.

It had been a long meeting now that there were six members in the group, rather than three. And it was the newer two members who were causing problems.

"It's getting worse," said Shakira, watching Elaheh, Queen of Tawazun, walk out of the room with a haughty swish of the traditional robes she always wore. "It cannot go on like this."

The cause of Elaheh's abrupt departure—Xander, the newly appointed King of Sharq Havilah—appeared not in the least perturbed. He stood out of earshot on the terrace, hands thrust into his pockets, his habitual frown framing his handsome face.

Roshan also looked concerned as he finished his coffee

and pushed away the empty cup. "They need to learn to work together."

"I agree with Shakira," said Zavian. "This can't be allowed to continue. Their enmity could undermine everything we are working towards, the peace we've worked so hard to create."

"They can't seem to stand being in the same room together!" said Amir. "They're impossible."

"They need to learn to work together," repeated Roshan thoughtfully, his joined fists tapping against his lips as he surveyed his brother, chatting to one of the blushing maids. "My brother is not accustomed to being conciliatory."

"And nor is Elaheh," murmured Shakira.

Zavian thumped the table lightly. "Then they should work together on the Havilah-Tawazun infrastructure project. Just the two of them. It is a subject dear to both their hearts—"

"If they have hearts," muttered Amir.

"And so they will have to learn to work together in order for the project to succeed." Zavian turned to Roshan.

"What do you think, Roshan? Will your brother be able to work with Elaheh?"

Roshan bit his lip and Shakira could see he was conflicted. He loved his brother but was concerned at Xander's controlling nature and apparent inability to compromise. He also felt guilty for having abdicated in order to marry her, leaving Xander king of the country he so dearly loved. "He'll have to. I'll talk to him."

Shakira squeezed Roshan's hand and shot him a warm, supportive smile. "And I'll talk to Elaheh," she said. She turned to Zavian and Amir. "Leave it with us, we'll make them see they *have* to work together, for all our sakes."

Zavian and Amir exchanged relieved glances.

"Thank you," said Amir. "There's no alternative. They *must* work together or else everything is compromised." He sighed. "They're both fine people... *separately*. It's when they're together there's a problem." He shrugged.

"Trouble is, they're opposites," added Zavian.

As the three men went to join Xander, Shakira remained seated, her hand on her swollen belly. She heard Queen Elaheh's helicopter take off. Her heart sank.

The meeting had been a near disaster. Whenever Xander had spoken, Elaheh had visibly bristled and had given a cutting reply which Xander had ignored. It was like watching some kind of reality TV show—with all the danger and sparkiness and none of the humor. It chilled her to the core. She'd witnessed enough conflict and dissension in her life to know what harm it could do. She just hoped that Zavian's plan would work, despite the fact he'd got the heart of the problem wrong.

"Trouble is," murmured Shakira to herself, "Xander and Elaheh aren't opposites—they're too much alike."

CHAPTER 1

One week later...

"That woman is becoming *more* impossible, if anything!" Xander scowled back at the group he and his brother, Roshan, had left behind in the hall of the desert hunting lodge in which the kings of Havilah always met. "Can't we do something about her?"

Roshan sat down and put his feet on the coffee table. He hooked his arms across the back of the chair, looking for all the world like the king of the country he was no longer king of.

"What do you suggest?" he asked facetiously. "Have her deposed and exiled from her own country? Come on, Xander. We *have* to work with her. She's too important."

Xander couldn't take his eyes off the petite woman who still held court over Amir, Zavian and Shakira. "*And* she knows it, *and* she's taking full advantage of it."

Roshan followed Xander's gaze. "Shakira gets on well with her. She says she's really smart." He shrugged. "I don't believe she's being deliberately provocative. She's simply a woman who knows what she wants."

"And no doubt she wants a husband. I pity the poor man *she* marries."

"Apparently, she's showing no inclination to marry. Quite the opposite, in fact. Shame really. She'd be a great match for you."

Xander was so incensed he couldn't speak immediately. Roshan gave him a double take and then calmly took another sip of his coffee.

"Perfect," Roshan added with a smile.

"You're enjoying this, aren't you?"

Roshan's grin widened. "Maybe. It makes a change from me being the subject of matrimonial gossip and conjecture."

"Well you can stop conjecturing about me and Elaheh. She's made it quite clear she can't stand me."

Roshan tilted his head to one side and pursed his lips. "I'm not so sure. Sometimes, I think the way she looks at you and makes you a target of her cutting remarks reveals an uncommon interest."

Xander tossed down his phone in irritation and looked over Roshan's shoulder at the woman in question. "You're crazy," he muttered, his eyes lingering on the upright way Elaheh stood, her back ramrod straight, and her thick dark hair pulled severely into an elaborate hairstyle. For a moment he wondered how long it would be when released from its tight bindings—if it were ever released. He couldn't imagine Queen Elaheh ever being anything other than perfectly groomed. He smiled to himself; she probably went to sleep with her hair like that. But it did have a certain luster and fullness suggesting it was long. It probably fell to her bottom. His eyes lingered at where that bottom would be, hidden beneath a swathe of white robes. Then she turned to him and caught his eye. And for a moment their gazes clashed and tangled, and there was a flare of something he couldn't put his finger on. In ordinary circumstances he'd have known what to call it—attraction. But these were definitely not ordinary circumstances, and she was definitely no ordinary woman. This was a woman who hated him, he reminded himself. A woman who couldn't speak to him without either insulting or criticizing him. A woman who he hated right back.

He scowled at her and she looked away. Xander turned back to Roshan. "I repeat, Elaheh has no interest in me, and I have no interest in her."

"But you will marry, won't you?"

"Of course. I know my duty. I will marry and produce heirs as is expected."

Roshan nodded. "Good. Shakira asked me to ask you if you had anyone in mind."

His gaze shifted to Elaheh and, annoyed at his weakness, he glared at her back. "Yes, as it happens and she's nothing like Elaheh."

Roshan raised his eyebrow. "You have? Who?"

Xander ran a finger around his collar as if it were suddenly too tight. "A friend of mine from university. She's an expert on historical architecture. She'd be most suitable."

"Most suitable? That doesn't sound like a match made in heaven."

Xander glared at his brother. "We can't all fall in love like you did with Shakira. That's a one-off."

Roshan shook his head. "No, it's not. Look at Amir and Ruby, look at Zavian and Gabrielle. Two other couples who are crazy about each other.

It was Xander's turn to grunt. "I don't do crazy. I don't *want* crazy." He cleared his throat. "Ashley is an academic —more interested in her feminist research than falling crazy in love."

"Sounds a riot," murmured Roshan, rolling his eyes.

"There you go again! 'Riot', 'crazy'—these are things I refuse to have in my life."

Silence stretched and thickened and Xander knew what his brother was thinking.

"You used to, Xander, when you were young. Before—"

Xander shot his hand out, his palm flat against his brother's words, determined to stop their flow. He refused to hear any more. "Don't go there, Roshan."

Roshan pressed his lips together and nodded slowly. "Okay, for now. But you have to some time, if you're ever to move forward."

Xander shifted his gaze away from Roshan, away from Elaheh, to the window which looked out toward the empty desert—a constant reminder of everything he didn't wish to remember. Move forward? Xander felt as if he'd moved backward. Back to this place, his country, the only place in the world it seemed he couldn't avoid, and which was full of harsh memories which he was deter- mined to suppress. He gave an ambiguous grunt, which Roshan took for agreement.

"Okay. So this Ashley is a possibility. Why don't you describe to me your ideal wife and Shakira and I'll see if we can't help with some introductions."

"I'm fine with Ashley."

"Does she know yet?"

Xander shook his head once. "But she will. She's coming to visit in a few months."

"Okay. So I hope that goes well for you. But, in the mean time, let's see if we can drum up some competition for Ashley. Describe your perfect woman." Roshan sat back expectantly.

Xander blinked as he continued to gaze at the distant horizon while his mind was suddenly filled with Elaheh's face. Whatever she looked like, he told himself firmly, he wanted the opposite.

Xander suddenly remembered the way Elaheh's mouth was level to his chest as she looked up to him. Her breath against his neck had been like the scorching simoom desert winds, whittling away whatever it hits to its essence. He cleared his throat.

"My wife will be tall," said Xander, walking briskly to the desk he was using. He picked up a report, looked at it without reading it and then placed it firmly on a pile of outgoing correspondence. But the paperwork failed to remove the vision of Elaheh's eyes, bright against her dark skin. He glanced up at Roshan who was observing him closely. "And pale. Definitely pale."

"Pale?" Roshan raised an eyebrow. "So, not a local woman then?"

Xander shook his head and looked at the paperwork again. "No."

"Anything else?"

Xander tossed down the paper, put his hands in his pockets and looked into the mid-distance. Elaheh's beautiful lips rarely settled into their natural shape. They were always moving, always communicating her thoughts. "Quiet. Not much to say for herself but when she does speak…" He smiled to himself at the thought of Elaheh's voice. He always felt it was perhaps the one true thing about her that she wasn't able to disguise. It spoke more truly than the words she uttered, and its dulcet tones never failed to bypass all his objections to her and hit the target he managed to hide from everyone else. "Her voice will be soft, musical and seductive." So, perhaps his ideal wife wouldn't be the exact opposite. Okay to let that slip in, maybe, but he had to be firm on everything else. His future wife must be the opposite to Elaheh in every other way.

"That's some list. Anything else?"

Xander turned to his older brother. "Curvaceous, large breasts." He turned away. "I like large breasts." He paused for a moment as he imagined Elaheh's small breasts. "And" —he swept his hand in a careless gesture—"you know, easy company. I don't want anyone who's hard work." He picked up a book and riffled through it for something to do.

"You're very definite in your views. I'm guessing you're describing this Ashley person."

And, to his surprise, Xander realized he was. He narrowed his gaze onto his paperwork, comparing the two women in his mind's eye. The one, Elaheh, he couldn't stand. That much was obvious. The other, Ashley, he got on well with. She was beautiful and everything he'd just described. His frown deepened. Then why didn't she arouse his passions like Elaheh did?

He slammed the book shut. And that was exactly how he wanted it. If there was no passion, there was no pain. A simple equation, and one he fully intended to cling to.

"Don't bother looking for a wife for me, Roshan. I'll sort that out for myself."

Roshan sighed. "Ashley."

"Yes. Dr Ashley Maitland and myself will create a formidable team. We're friends. That's a good start."

"Maybe," said Roshan.

Xander couldn't ignore the doubt which was redolent in that one word.

"No *maybe* about it."

Roshan grimaced. "I don't think the woman of your dreams can be described in such specific terms. You sound so sure about what you want."

"I am. Because I know exactly what I *don't* want. Or, should I say, *who* I don't want to marry, nor have anything to do with."

"Ah," replied Roshan, the light suddenly dawning on his face. "I see."

Xander grunted. "Good. And so do I. When I look at Elaheh, when I hear her carping on at me, I know exactly that she is nothing, absolutely nothing, like the person I wish to marry." He sat in a chair, feeling suddenly defeated, and looked bleakly at Roshan. He swore with fierce exaggeration under his breath. "Elaheh is a woman to drive a man out of his mind! If I have to spend any more time with her it'll be too much. If I have to listen to her bossy ideas, I'll go round the bend. In short, brother, keep me as far away from her as possible. Because if you don't, I won't answer for the consequences."

"Oh dear," groaned Roshan, taking a few steps away,

and pulling out his phone. "Look, I have to go. But I'll be in touch."

"This is sudden. I thought you were going to stay for dinner."

Roshan gave a quick smile. "Change of plan."

Xander frowned as an unwelcome suspicion formed in the back of his mind. Something he'd said had made Roshan change his mood, and his plans. He mentally went over the previous conversation. He couldn't move over one particular sentence. He groaned. "You haven't, have you?"

Roshan smiled, too brightly, his hand gripping the door. "Haven't what?"

Xander tilted his head to one side and narrowed his eyes, his gaze never leaving Roshan's. "You know," he said, in his best menacing voice. "You haven't arranged anything between me and Elaheh, have you."

He didn't raise his intonation at the end of the sentence. It was a statement, not a question.

"Well, funny you should say that."

Xander didn't think it funny. He remained silent as he watched his brother carefully.

"As it happens, I spoke to Amir and Zavian the other day and we're all agreed. The best way to progress the infrastructure and communications project between Sharq Havilah and Tawazun is to have the two rulers discuss it—person to person." Roshan gestured helplessly. "That way, there will be less going back and forth, and it can progress more quickly." He gripped the handle, released his grip and then gripped it again. He looked positively nervous, which made Xander nervous. Roshan never looked nervous. "There will just be the two of you. It'll be easier that way."

Xander threw the nearest file at Roshan but it landed with a thud against a closed door. And all he could here was laughter from his brother as he walked away. "Definitely easier!" Roshan shouted through the closed door.

"For you maybe," roared Xander, throwing himself into a chair and looking at the paperwork which now lay strewn across the room. "For you," he added. "But not for me."

ELAHEH STOOD in the entrance to the ancient desert hunting lodge—the site of all the meetings of the kings and queens of Havilah—and felt a sinking in her stomach as she folded up the strange note and pushed it into her pocket and out of her mind.

It wasn't the first such note, but she'd make sure it was the last. Just not now. This morning she had greater concerns than a letter threatening her safety. She glanced at her faithful vizier, Abzari, who stood to one side, his silent, reassuring presence appreciated in this strange world of politics and posturing in which she'd found herself. And then she looked straight ahead, summoning all her reserves of strength to meet her visitor. For it wasn't the usual meeting of all the kings and queens, today she'd be meeting only one. And he was late.

She filled her lungs with the hot, dry air of the vast desert which surrounded them. To the others, dwellers in cities, it must seem foreign, she thought. But, to her, born and bred in the nomadic tent cities of the Bedouin, it was home. It was her world and one she understood. That was why she wanted to meet here, rather than the city state of Sharq Havilah—with all its modern towers and busy streets—or her own palace in Tawazun. Here, she had only one thing to contend with, one person to control: King Xander of Sharq Havilah. He was proving unresisting to her demands. But she'd make sure he did as she wanted. In the end.

The hum of the approaching helicopter was like an annoying insect at first, gradually growing louder until the throbbing of its blades filled the air, overtaking the silence with its unwelcome noise. Inwardly, Elaheh flinched; outwardly her eyes narrowed a little. How was it that even the approach of the man was enough to disturb her equilibrium?

She adjusted her scarf around her head as the helicopter hovered above them and descended into the vast courtyard, sand and dust billowing all around them. She didn't retreat. It wasn't in her nature.

Xander stepped out of the helicopter with his head down, and strode over to the entrance of the desert palace, his advisors following him. After shooting a narrowed glance at her, his gaze rose and took in the hunting lodge—once a palace fortress—with its ancient mysterious engravings around the entrance and uncompromising red-stone facade designed to repel invaders. Elaheh just wished it was strong enough to repel Xander.

It wasn't until he came close to her that he met her gaze, which hadn't wavered from him. Most of the time all she had to do to command people was look at them. Her father had noted that, even as a small child, she had a fierce gaze from which people shrank. It had been her curse, as it had repelled people she hadn't wished to repel, but it had also proved, in the long run, to be her savior and protector.

"Xander," she said shortly as he stood before her. She was annoyed to have to look up so far. He was taller than the other kings. And she had to steel herself, grit her teeth to face those eyes. She hated the flutter she felt when she looked into those narrowed, stern, controlling black eyes.

"Elaheh," he replied with equal brevity.

She waited for the traditional words of greeting. But, as there were none, she turned with a sweep of her gowns and entered the hall.

Even though she couldn't see him, she sensed his eyes on her. It was like a tickling feeling traveling along her spine. She could feel the fine hairs on the back of her neck prickle and she shivered slightly.

She stopped in the hallway and turned to him.

"Cold?" he asked, looking around. "I guess it is cool in here if you're not accustomed to air conditioning. And I don't believe you use it in your palace, do you?"

Anger sparked inside. One, he'd noticed her shiver. She didn't want him looking at her intently enough to notice her shiver. And two, he couldn't help but be negative about her ancient palace and traditional way of life.

"It's not necessary. I *guess*," she said, emphasizing the slang word which *she* never used, but which Xander often did. "If you spend most of your life away from your home, you don't feel you belong here. And, if that is how you feel, perhaps you should leave." She flicked her hand dismissively. "Perhaps you should return to the UK or US or wherever you're from, and your air-conditioned offices and superficial lifestyle."

He bowed his head to hers, his eyes fierce, but she refused to flinch. "Oh, Elaheh," he said, and his warm breath swept over her cheeks and neck, causing yet another round of prickles. "I belong. Just as you do. And I'm afraid I'm not going anywhere. I'm King of Sharq Havilah and there's nothing you can do about it."

"More's the pity," she said between gritted teeth.

He withdrew and those dark eyes held a spark of humor. She hated that even more. "You don't mean it. After all, who would you spar with then?"

The anger became something like fury. She could feel it bubble up but, before she could express herself, he'd turned on his heel, hands in pockets in his usual careless, relaxed manner, and walked toward the meeting room.

There was nothing she could do except follow. She hated following anyone, let alone a man who could make her so angry that she found the vibrations of encounters with him continued to reverberate long after they'd gone their separate ways.

They took their places around the medieval table—its heavily polished patina, together with the over-sized richly-colored rug which covered the stone-flagged floor, creating a warmth to the cavernous hall. In recent times the table had had to seat six kings and queens, rather than the original three Havilahi kings. But, today, there were just the two of them.

Elaheh waved away her maid. She wanted to get down to work. She didn't want this meeting to go on a moment longer than it had to.

Xander raised an eyebrow as he accepted a cup of coffee—an Italian espresso, Elaheh noted disapprovingly. "You're not having a coffee?" he asked.

She shook her head. "I'd rather we get down to business. The sooner we begin, the sooner we can go our separate ways."

He sat back in his chair and sipped his coffee, his eyes never leaving her. Despite herself, she could feel a heat rising in her. She never blushed. Somehow she willed it away.

"You're not welcoming time *alone* with me, are you?"

How he managed to place such loaded meaning on the word "alone" defeated her. She placed her hands calmly together and eyed him in silence for a few moments. That usually did it. But not, it seemed in Xander's case. He looked as cool and unperturbed as if, she imagined, he were sharing a morning coffee with friends at the beach. Not that she'd ever been able—or wanted, she reminded herself—to do such things.

"No," she said. "So I suggest we begin."

He shrugged as if he wasn't bothered either way.

His lack of seriousness ratcheted up her annoyance levels a further notch. It drove down any hint of a blush and the ice which usually ran through her veins returned. "You don't appear to care whether our discussions are successful, or not."

"Of course they'll be successful. Why wouldn't they be? We both want the same things."

"Which are?" It was her turn to raise a scornful eyebrow. "Perhaps you'd care to remind me."

"We both want what each other has."

Why did she feel he was talking about something far more personal than infrastructure projects? She stopped her mind from making an unwelcome swerve.

"I understand that you need my country's stability and

power and size to bolster your small, pocket-sized country," she replied. "And I have agreed to help with that. But we need little from you."

"You are being deliberately provocative." She'd rattled him. She knew she had, as he carefully replaced his cup into its saucer. His stance hadn't changed but he'd tensed his jaw. "You may be a large, powerful country, but Sharq Havilah has an infrastructure of which you can only dream."

"Phh! City skyscrapers, cell phone towers, and western boutiques." She made another derogatory sound. "These are not things my country needs."

"Then…" He leaned in to her. "Why are you here?"

She could have kicked herself. Her enmity for this infuriating man had driven her into a corner. He was right. She, and her country, needed his country's expertise to bring Tawazun into the modern age. She just didn't want to admit it.

She decided to take the easy route out and take his words at face value. "I am here, because of the treaty I signed with the three countries of Havilah, and with Jazira. I am here because I said I would be."

"You are here, Elaheh, because you need my help. And, so I suggest you quit attempting to antagonize me—which you won't succeed at, by the way."

They glared at each other in stalemate for a few moments. The air crackled between them but with what, Elaheh couldn't describe. There was animosity, but mixed in with that was an array of other feelings and emotions which left her confused and bewildered. And she couldn't afford to be either of those things now. She wanted to push him away, to slap his face, to wrestle him to the floor as she used to her cousins. That thought lingered and changed into a very uncousin-like image. It was Elaheh who turned away first, and opened the laptop.

She cleared her throat. "Item one on the agenda is telecommunications." She looked up at him, over the laptop. "I understand you have some expertise here."

"Indeed. And you need it, don't you?" A smile tweaked his lips, as if he'd won the first battle. He may have, but he wasn't going to win them all, she'd make sure of that.

She licked her lips, as she tried to form the words of capitulation—of admitting that she needed him. They refused to come.

"And then we'll move to item two," she said. "Your country's access to mine, over the mountains."

His smile fell. She had him there.

"I assume your country's need to access my country and all its unspoiled heritage and cultural riches is still of interest to you?" She pushed the point home.

He gave one short, sharp nod of the head. Good. They were even again.

"Then let's begin."

SHE WAS IMPOSSIBLE. Of all the women he'd ever met—and he'd met plenty—Queen Elaheh of Tawazun had to be the most obstinate, the coldest, the angriest and the most intractable that it had ever been his misfortune to meet. Sure, she was intelligent and beautiful. But she wielded those God-given gifts as weapons, and with painfully accurate aim.

He was weary of battling with her. At the end of another hard-driven bargain, he stood up.

"Where are you going?" she asked sharply. "We haven't finished here yet."

"You might not have, but I have. I need a break."

"You can have one here."

"No, I can't."

"Why not?" she pursued. She was relentless. Didn't she ever quit?

He turned around, completely exasperated. "Because, Elaheh, I need a break from you!"

He hadn't meant to say it. Rudeness wasn't something he appreciated in others or himself.

She snapped her laptop closed and glared at him. "You, Xander, are rude and uncouth!"

"And you, Elaheh, are a trial to do business with!"

The silence was thick with anger. "A trial?" she said, between tight lips. She rose. "A trial?" she repeated, as she walked around the table towards him. "Do you want to know what a trial really is? It's being forced to work with someone like you. You have no idea what it's like to be a Bedouin, no idea of our culture, our life, and yet you return to your place of birth, take up the crown and pretend you are one of us. You're *not* one of us, and nothing will ever make you one."

There, she'd just done it—hit the bullseye with the point of her rapier sword. He felt the sharp thrust at his innermost pain distantly. He'd spent his whole life covering it with layer upon layer of numbness and indifference, topped with the visible layers of arrogance and lazy charm. It fooled everyone except his brother. And he couldn't believe it hadn't fooled Elaheh. What she'd done, she'd done by instinct alone. Killer instinct.

He narrowed his gaze, trying to reduce the amount she

could see. She advanced on him as if scenting his weakness. She was close now, so close he could see the flecks of gold in her dark eyes—eyes that he'd first thought were like tiger's eyes. That was before he knew that there were more ways than one in which she resembled a tiger, and none of them were attractive. He gritted his teeth, trying to keep control of his temper.

"Stop it, Elaheh, before one of us says something we'll regret."

"I'm not stopping anything!" Her eyes were aflame and she did, indeed, look unstoppable. "I'm being forced to deal with one such as you—a king by default only, a foreigner!"

"Believe me, Elaheh, I've a million things I'd prefer to be doing right now, and none of them would be with you. You are the worst, coldest, most charm-free woman it's ever been my misfortune to meet! No wonder none of the other kings wanted to marry you!"

The formidable look melted away and for a few long, interminable seconds he saw a look of vulnerability and hurt which mingled with his own and made everything a whole lot worse.

He reached out and touched her arm, instinctively needing to make contact, to mend the hurt he'd inflicted. "I'm sorry, I didn't mean that."

Her beautiful eyes now glittered like gold with tears that didn't fall. She shook her head. "You *did* mean it. You're too honest *not* to speak the truth. That much, at least, I know about you." She pulled her arm away from him, looking at it as if his touch had burned her.

He reached out again for her. He needed to take away her pain, he needed to bridge the gap that had widened like a treacherous ravine between them. But she tore her arm away and rubbed it. "Don't touch me. I hate being touched." This was getting worse.

She backed away from him as if she was frightened of what he might do. He held up his hands. "Elaheh, look, I'm so sorry. I didn't mean to hurt you, or frighten you. You must know that I'm not the hurting kind."

She walked quickly to the door.

"Please, Elaheh, don't let's leave it like this. I apologize for my stupid comments. I didn't mean them. It's just you drive me crazy."

She slowly turned around. "That's not my problem."

He panicked at the thought that she'd walk away and their talks would stall. "No, you're right. But we can get through this."

"Of course. Did you think I was leaving? Not before business has been completed. I, Xander, am a professional. I don't put the personal before business. And neither should you."

He watched her leave the room with a rustle of her robes, her scent lingering on the air. He took a deep breath of it. At first he'd thought it too strong, not as subtle as a French perfume, but the rich fragrance had filtered into his system somehow and brought a frisson of unwanted emotion with it. What kind he couldn't have said, as he quickly stifled it.

He needed to take a leaf out of her book and push the personal back where it belonged. Nowhere.

ELAHEH SMILED at her maid ruefully as she entered her room, instantly allowing the brittle veneer with which she protected herself to melt away, as she accepted a cool drink. She shrugged off her robes, revealing the loose shift dress she wore beneath. Some people wore jeans and shorts under their robes, but she preferred a smart dress based on the traditional. It was white, as were all her clothes. She favored it.

But she didn't take a sip from her glass. She was too wound up. What Xander said had hurt. She felt the rustle in her pocket and withdrew the folded-up letter. This time she read it properly and she noticed the threat at the end. But more than that, she was concerned about how it had reached her. No one, apart from her close circle of inner advisers knew where she was. She looked around at the maid, and the others who worked close by and suddenly felt distrustful of everyone. And, for the first time in her adult life, she felt scared.

CHAPTER 2

"So," said Xander, smoothing the map of their two countries across the table which stood between them.

"So," repeated Elaheh warily, as she looked at Xander, not the map. The map she knew inside out, Xander she didn't. She needed to understand him if she was going to work with him.

He glanced up, his dark eyes impenetrable and cold. She almost flinched under their gaze but knew it wouldn't be visible to him. She'd spent long years ensuring no one would know what was going on in her brain, or in her heart. It was her only defense against the world of men in which she lived.

He shifted his gaze back to the map and tapped his index finger on one particular place. She couldn't help notice that his fingernails were clean and buffed. The man was immaculate. She gritted her teeth. She liked immaculate. It was free of complications and chaos. Usually.

"The new route between our countries will of course, follow the old Bedouin trail across the mountains."

She didn't shift her gaze. "It will be expensive and take years to complete."

"Maybe, but our countries can both afford it and will be the richer for the connection."

She looked up and held his gaze. "Your tourism trade will obviously benefit by the drawcard of our traditional culture and ancient buildings. Things your modern country with all its glass towers and technology cannot supply." She sat back and folded her arms, content her barbed comment would find its target, that it would be felt somewhere behind Xander's cool, polished exterior.

"And yours," he said firmly, leaning forward and resting his forearms on his thighs as he lifted his frowning face closer to hers, "will gain access to the sea, and our port, things you've never had before."

"The lack of which has kept us safe for centuries," she snapped, refusing to be bested.

"Safe, because no one was interested in a country without access to the sea." He sat back again, eyeing her intently. "Look, if you despise my country's modernity, you have the choice to remain in the dark ages." He shrugged. "I really don't care. Your country will benefit far more than mine."

A flare of anger shot through her at the injustice of this statement. "You lie, Xander, and there is no point us working together if you continue to do that." She waggled her finger at him. "You know exactly what you'll be getting—a percentage of all our goods and oil which will flow through your port, as well as the tourism which my country will attract."

Suddenly he reached forward and grabbed her waggling finger and gripped it tightly. "Don't. Ever. Do. That. Again!"

She pulled away in surprise. "I shall do exactly as I like."

"If you treat me like a child, I'll walk away."

"Exactly as a child would!"

They glared at each other in a fiery impasse, broken only by the insistent ringing from Xander's phone. With an irritated grunt, Xander slid the phone off the table into his hand, rose and walked away. "Yes!"

Elaheh inhaled a shaky breath of relief as Xander walked away. She could withstand pressure from opposing forces whether they be her ministers, visiting diplomats, or family, all intent on imposing their will on someone they believed to be a weak woman. But what she couldn't stand was Xander being close to her. It was personal, it was intense, and it got through to her like nothing else could.

She needed air. She went to the window and pushed it open, relieved as the dry heat flooded the chill, air-conditioned room and filled her lungs. She didn't know how Xander and the other kings could stand such artificial conditions. She needed to feel the desert air on her face, and in her body, in order to survive; she needed to feel the essence of the country in her veins in order to live.

She half-listened to Xander's conversation which mainly consisted of grunts on his part. It took her a little while to work out that it was his brother, Roshan, on the other end of the line. It was only after Xander's grunts appeared to be in the affirmative—he'd agreed to something, but she had no idea what—that he finished his call, tossed the phone back on the table and sat down again.

He appeared conflicted as he thrust his fingers through his hair. His lips formed a straight line, as did his gaze as it shot directly at her. Bullseye. "Sit down, Elaheh. We have to stop sniping and get on with business."

"Is that what your brother told you?" She didn't wait for an answer because she knew both Xander and Roshan were correct. Whatever she'd said, whatever Xander had said, they both needed this project to be a success as it would ultimately benefit both their countries.

Xander didn't bother to respond but flipped open the laptop, opened a document and turned it around to her.

"What's this?" she asked suspiciously.

"An initial roading report. I suggest we accept its recommendations and immediately requisition a full and complete report including resources and timelines to let us know what we're in for, so we can get started. Agreed?"

She restrained herself to a simple black look. "Not yet. I haven't read it."

She took the laptop and began to read, aware of his impatience. Despite that, she took her time and read every word. She nodded as she closed the laptop and pushed it over the table, back to him. "Agreed," she said simply. She was surprised to see a change in his attitude. Gone was the coldness, he even looked amused. It made her less amused.

"What do you find so funny?" she said in her haughtiest voice.

He shrugged lightly and his lips quirked briefly. "You."

"I am *not* amusing."

"True. You're far from amusing, much too stern for

that. But you *are* funny. Unintentionally so. And that's what makes it even funnier."

"You talk nonsense, Xander. Is that what your Ivy League education got you? Is that what networking with all your slick friends makes you?" She stood up. "For want of anything solid to say, you turn the tables and try to make fun of me? Is that all you can do? You should be ashamed!"

With that, she stalked out of the conference room and swept through ancient corridors to the suite of rooms which would be hers for the next few days, until their discussions were complete. Once in the room, she dismissed her maids, flung open all the window onto the central courtyard and paced her room, trying to calm herself while all the time winding herself up more by the thought of his face, his eyes, laughing at her.

If there was one thing she hated, it was being laughed at.

XANDER REGRETTED ALLOWING himself to give in to his impulse to laugh at her. She had looked like a young girl absorbed in the technicalities of the report and it had been that which had touched him. But when she'd caught his gaze and her expression had instantly changed back to the fierce mask of before, she'd been correct—he'd lied to defend himself.

It was ridiculous, all this parrying and thrusting all the time, like some kind of jousting match. As well as being exhausting it was fruitless and pointless, exactly as Roshan had said. They needed to put it behind them and get on with things. Despite that, Xander suspected that the kings and Shakira had put them together in order to resolve their personal differences, as well as political.

And Xander knew deep down that Elaheh was right. He had had the type of education which depended more on verbal parrying, than integrity and honesty. Roshan's words ran through his head. Despite the fact his elder brother was married and living on the island nation of Jazira now, and very happily so, he kept a watchful eye on Xander. And, despite Xander's initial irritation, he was thankful for Roshan's continuing, steadying and watchful support. Xander hadn't realized how much he didn't know about being king. But it had been Roshan's final advice which he'd found hardest to consider. Roshan had suggested Xander imagine, for two days, that Elaheh was the most desirable woman in the world and that he should charm her accordingly.

He glared at the laptop. He'd been checking through the documentation trying to figure out a way in which he didn't need her as much as she needed him. But there was no way. He snapped it shut and jumped up. They all needed this project to get underway and Roshan was right, Xander was being too obstinate. But it was her, Elaheh. She rubbed him up the wrong way. He'd go see her and charm her. He could do it.

ELAHEH LOOKED AROUND SHARPLY at the knock on her door. She didn't move immediately. Her staff knew that she always spent this hour in contemplation. It had been how she'd spent most of her youth. What had begun as an escape, she now appreciated as a time to get her thoughts together and re-charge. Whoever was knocking would go away, she thought and closed her eyes once more.

But it came again. She ground her teeth. It must be someone new. She'd sort him out. She opened the door, ready to give the person a mouthful but was stunned to see Xander holding a bottle of champagne and two champagne flutes and even more shockingly, a smile on those usually stern lips.

"What are you doing here?" she asked, letting the door swing open in her surprise.

He waggled the bottle and glasses. "If you let me in, I'll tell you." A gust of wind caught the door and it appeared she'd opened it further. "May I?"

She was so stunned that when he stepped forward, she stepped back and allowed him to enter. Various scenarios ran through her mind. Maybe something had happened. There could be no other reason why he'd appeared.

She looked into the corridor at her security guard who sat not far away. She opened her hands in question but the man shrugged. He obviously had no clue either. She closed the door. Whatever Xander had to say, it was obviously important and so was best heard without an audience.

He looked around as he walked across to the sideboard where he set down the glasses. "This is a nice suite of rooms. I've never been here before." He turned to her with a grin which set her pulse racing.

"What do you want? What's happened?"

He cocked his head to one side, his smile slipping into an even more seriously sexy quirk of the lips. "Why should anything need to have happened in order for us to share a bottle of champagne?"

She folded her arms and pursed her lips. "Maybe the world has to end first?"

His sexy grin slipped a little and he looked momentarily unsure. She felt a flare of confidence and walked up to him. She reached out to grab the bottle but he was too quick for her and his hand shot out and took hold of hers. She jumped as if an electric shock had run through her. And, just as if the shock melded their fists together, his tightened around hers as the unsureness fell away, replaced by a very male satisfied smile.

"Can't wait, hey?"

Even more insolently, he ran his thumb across the back of her hand. But for some reason her body didn't respond to her thoughts but to an instinct she hadn't known she possessed. And that instinct was focused on a sensation which travelled like a row of dominoes knocking each other over, as they raised the hairs on her arm and shot to other parts of her body. She felt torn, broken, unable to remember the last time a person had touched her so innocently, and yet so intimately. A gasp caught in her throat as she felt tears rise from a fount which she'd thought was dry.

He frowned but his grip held. "What is it, Ela?"

Her confusion of feelings was compounded by him using a nickname for her, a name she'd only ever been called by her mother. The memory of her mother burst into her head, clearing it, and she tore her hand from his grip.

She held her hand up as if it were burning. She tried to speak but nothing emerged. She licked her lips. "Don't call me that." Her voice sounded hoarse to her ears. She half-stepped, half-staggered away from Xander. She shook her head, trying to rid it of the memories which had risen, trying to re-find the woman she'd made herself into. "Don't call me that," she repeated, stronger now. She stepped forward once more, grabbed the bottle and walked across the room. She opened the door to her bathroom and poured the champagne into the basin.

When she returned she found Xander hadn't moved. But when she caught his eye, he did. "And pouring away a decent bottle of Moet is your way of telling me you don't drink champagne?"

She nodded. "It seemed easiest."

He raised an incredulous eyebrow. "It would have been far easier, not to say less wasteful, to say, 'I don't drink champagne, Xander'."

She shrugged. "It's the same message. I've never drunk alcohol and I never intend to."

"Fair enough. So, tell me, what do you do to celebrate?"

"Celebrate?" She shook her head, suddenly aware that she couldn't remember the last time she'd celebrated anything, not for her personally, anyway. There had been no birthday parties for her and her younger sister after her mother had been forced to leave. "And what exactly are we celebrating?"

"The fact that, despite a bumpy beginning to our friendship—"

"*Friendship?*" she interrupted.

"Friendship," he repeated firmly. "Despite that, we've managed to get through a whole day without killing each other. Surely that's something to celebrate?"

"We're celebrating the fact that we haven't killed each other." His lips quirked again and it was as if a string was pulled inside her. The feeling wasn't unpleasant. And then a strange thing happened, a bubble of laughter emerged from somewhere deep inside of her. She didn't know who was most surprised. She blushed. Another new experience.

"Come on," Xander said with a smile. "Let's push out the boat and find some sparkling water to celebrate something else."

"What?"

Xander ducked his head close to hers and for once those eyes held something other than cool separation. "Your smile," he said. "It's something to behold." He pulled away. "And somehow I doubt many people have beheld it. *That* is definitely worth celebrating."

It seemed easier to follow him outside. Besides, it was cooler there, she persuaded herself. And she desperately needed something to take the heat out of her blush.

She took a deep breath and followed him to the evening bar where the kings went to relax at the end of a day. It was an ancient castle, and fitted out to meet the exact requirements of visiting royalty, but no one lived there. It was too important. It was positioned dead center of Havilah, and the only place where all three Havilahi countries met. It was also a half-way point between Sharq Havilah and her own country of Tawazun.

The bar wasn't manned and Xander rummaged in its cupboards and withdrew a bottle of sparkling water and two glasses in triumph.

"Now the bar *is* a place I am familiar with," he said, pouring them both a glass.

"I'm sure," she said, accepting the glass. And she was—

there was no doubt he looked totally at home in this social space, in a way that she never was.

He indicated a barstool and, despite protestations gathering in her mind, she sat. As he took a seat next to her, his leg brushed hers. She stared at the bubbles popping in her glass.

"So, Ela, what do you normally do on a Friday night?"

She frowned, her attention still on the effervescent liquid. It was easiest. She felt out of her depth. "The same as I do every other night. I work, I read, I pray, and then I go to bed."

He let out a low whistle. "You really know how to enjoy yourself."

She bristled, and turned to him. "I am queen. There is no time for frivolity."

"I had assumed there would be more." He took a sip of his mineral water and grimaced. "I certainly wouldn't have taken this job on, if I thought I could no longer enjoy myself."

"That is because you are a dilettante. You were not born to be king, and unless you take your new role seriously, you will not *continue* to be king."

To her chagrin, he gave a slow lop-sided smile, and took another leisurely sip of water. "You really know how to flatter a guy."

"I *really* don't," she said in a tone echoing his own. "And I *really* don't intend to." She raised herself up on the barstool, in as regal a position as she could and glared at him. "Flattery is for the weak. And I am not weak."

He still didn't appear perturbed by her response. He simply shook his head and thrust his fingers through his short hair. He gave a gruff laugh. "I can see I'm going to have my work cut out with you."

"Work?" She frowned as a flurry of suspicions jostled for space in her mind. She settled on the obvious one. "Did Roshan suggest all of this?" She studied his reaction intently and realized she was correct. "He told you to flirt with me, didn't he?" The more guilty Xander's expression became, the more steely her resolve grew. "Well, you can tell him from me, that I am not a woman to be flirted with."

"You don't say," said Xander wearily.

"I *do* say. So why don't we talk business instead."

Xander sighed and shifted around to face her.

"What I think you fail to realize, Ela—"

"Don't call me Ela."

"Is that I am not some lackey who you can order around. In case you didn't realize it I am also a king, who you need, whether you like it or not. Now, I understand you have not the first idea how to talk to me, but I suggest you learn, fast, because we have to work together. And I, for one, would prefer to make this a pleasurable experience."

She hadn't heard him speak so much in one go about things that weren't related to business. Arguments sprang into her mind that would contradict his words, but none of them would do because she realized he was right.

A smile glimmered on his lips. "You know, for all your sternness, when you are confused I can see your thoughts as clearly as the stars at night. It's quite sweet really."

"Now you've gone too far. I'm not, and nor will I ever be, sweet. But I do accept the fact that we need to work together. And..." She hesitated as she groped to find the correct word. "I suppose that, despite appearances I, too, would prefer an orderly meeting."

His smile turned into a broad grin. He lifted his glass to hers. "If I can't get fun, then orderly will do. It's a start. I'll drink to orderly."

As she brought her glass to his, he tapped them together.

He leaned in close to her. "And, you never know, I may persuade you to enjoy yourself."

She found herself smiling, despite her best intentions. "I'm not sure I would know even if I was." The words had tumbled out before her brain could filter them. And, as she saw his brow crease, she instantly regretted speaking without thinking. She had revealed something of herself.

With careful deliberation Xander pushed his empty glass onto the bar, and sat up straight, his arms lightly folded as he considered her. "Tell me, Ela, what happened to you to make you not understand enjoyment, to make you so scared to let go?"

She bit her lip and placed her glass back on the counter. She shot him a brief tight smile. "I think I'd better be calling it a night."

"And confirm my thoughts? That you are backing off because you're scared?"

In her best imperious voice she said, "I am tired, Xander, that is all." She would have been able to leave if he hadn't reached out and touched her hand. Just as before, it halted every thought, and stimulated every feeling, and there was nothing she could do.

"Ela, I don't know what happened to you, but you are queen now, you have total power, and no one can take that away from you. I am no threat to you, I can only help you, so why not stay, and talk? You might find you feel a little better."

All she could do was to look down at his hand and the thumb which caressed the back of hers. How could a simple caress create such havoc in every part of her body? She didn't dare look into his eyes, because then he would see her fear—naked and ugly. She swallowed. And then, from the depths of her, she summoned up the courage to meet his gaze. The smile was wiped from his face at what he saw.

"As you may know, my parents divorced and my mother died shortly afterwards."

Xander nodded. "I had heard."

"But what you might not know, Xander, is that my parents were opposite. My mother wanted fun. She enjoyed shopping, parties and..." She hesitated. "Over-indulging with alcohol... and other things. My father was traditional and did not approve." It was a mild description of how her father felt but she didn't care to elaborate. "He told me to watch and learn. And I did. I learned two things. My mother's rejection was absolute. As was her isolation. She wasn't allowed near me or my sister." She sucked in a deep breath. "She died alone...Not long after." She nearly stumbled but forced herself to continue, to admit the truth to Xander. "Accidental overdose was the verdict. It was hushed up of course. My father taught me well. There is no room in life for weakness, no room for error, especially if you rule a country, especially for a woman. That was the first thing I learned."

His grip tightened around her hands. He put his other hand on hers and squeezed it gently. "Hence no alcohol, hence a rigid control over yourself."

She shrugged. "I am who I am. Just as you are who you are. I don't think about the whys and wherefores. I am just me."

He brought their joined fists to his lips and kissed her fingertips, before releasing her hand. "And just you is enough. I *like* just you."

The tight wad she kept inside herself throbbed as if about to explode. She didn't even realize it was there anymore. The throbbing rose to her head and her temples. She rose and, uncharacteristically, rubbed her fingers across the forehead and stepped away. "I have to go now."

"Are you sure?" he asked. "Why not stay and we can discover more about each other?"

There was something in the way he said that which made her pause. For the first time since her confession she looked him straight in the eye and she didn't like what she saw there. It looked as if he'd won.

"You've got what you wanted, haven't you?" She cocked her head to one side as she thought things through. "That was what Roshan suggested wasn't it? Flirt with me, break me down. What is that Chinese proverb? Know your enemy?"

At least Xander had the grace not to lie outright. "Come on, Ela. It's not like that."

"Then what is it like? Do tell me, because I'm curious to know." He shrugged, and she knew she was correct. She shook her head. "I'm leaving."

"Stay, please. Besides we haven't finished our conversation. You didn't tell me the second thing you learned."

It took her a minute to figure out what he was referring to. "Ah, yes. The first was no alcohol and complete restraint, and the second? That's easy. The second is to never trust a man."

He frowned. "You can't believe that. We're not all the same, Ela."

"Don't call me Ela."

"Why not? It's your name."

"My mother called me Ela," she said, through a husky, barely controlled voice. "And I'm *not* that girl. *That* girl, *Ela*, died the day my mother left, forced away by my father, never to return. There is no Ela. My name is Elaheh. And if you, or Roshan, believe you can break me in order to control me, then you've both got another think coming."

She left the bar without a backward glance. But she wasn't the same person. Something had broken a little inside her when Xander had held her hand. Something that she hadn't even known she'd been forcing herself to hold together. But it had been there—tight inside of herself, curled up and made solid. And Xander had loosened it. It was chaos. It was fear. It was everything she didn't want. And she hated Xander for it.

CHAPTER 3

The next morning Elaheh rose before Xander. She was at work in the board room with her ministers around her. There would be no more tête-à-têtes, no more opportunities for Xander to try to break her. He might call it understanding her, but she knew the truth. He was only interested in one thing and that was nailing a deal which would benefit his country. And he was obviously prepared to soften her up in order to do it. She'd been weak yesterday; she didn't intend to be weak again.

When Xander entered the room, he raised an eyebrow in question. He gestured toward her ministers. "Is this necessary?"

"Yes. There's nothing more to discuss. We've agreed in principle, and now it's time to move onto the next level." She smiled coolly. "Please, feel free to summon your own ministers. The sooner we begin, the sooner we can both return home."

Xander gave a brief nod, his mouth grim, his fingers

tight around the back of his chair, betraying his displeasure. "Sure," he said.

Elaheh nodded in triumph. She'd put him back in his place and, with their staff around them, she'd ensure the remainder of their meeting would be strictly impersonal.

And so it was. The hours passed quickly as each detail was nailed down and approved. By the end of the morning, there was nothing further to discuss.

"Thank you everyone. I think we're finished here, now." She rose to follow her staff when Xander spoke from behind her.

"One moment, please, Elaheh," he said. She noticed he used her full name. Further proof, if required, that she had him where she wanted him.

She turned to him with an imperious glare. "What is it you want, Xander? Surely there's nothing to discuss that our executives can't deal with?"

"Yes, there is," he said firmly. Her heart sank. It seemed he was still resisting her will. "I wish to talk with you, in private. Just for a few minutes," he added.

She hesitated before giving him a curt nod. A few minutes she could cope with.

He opened the door for her and they walked out into the courtyard. It was almost spartan in design—unrelieved by trees, shrubs or flowers. Its simplicity dramatized its only feature—a perfect rectangular slice of water which reflected the brilliant blue of the sky. Instinctively, it seemed, he walked over to the water. She had the opposite instinct and sat on the stone seat by the door. He turned around and shook his head, as if in despair at her obstinacy. What he didn't understand was that if she didn't stand her ground, she'd lose the respect of every one around her. She'd learned that by watching her mother. There was no room for flexibility in this man's world in which she lived.

"Do I have to shout across the courtyard at you?" he called out.

"No, you may stand before me if you have something to say."

He shrugged and came and stood before her, closer than she'd have liked. She regretted requesting him to stand before her, while she sat. He had the advantage of height. She couldn't shift away easily, not without appearing to be intimidated. And there was no way she was ever going to appear intimidated by him.

Any further thought of intimidation vanished as she watched a strange expression move over his face. He was frowning as though displeased, but he blinked and his mouth twisted as though he were unsure of himself. She relaxed. This was going to be interesting.

"I wish to apologize, Elaheh. You were correct. Roshan did ask me to soften my stance towards you. But he didn't ask me to flirt with you, as you suggested. That was all my own, *brilliant,* idea." His emphasis showed that he no longer considered it to be brilliant.

She smiled. She hadn't thought that watching an arrogant, powerful man humble himself before her could be so entertaining. "Indeed. Far from brilliant. Insulting even, I'd go so far as to say."

He raised an eyebrow, his expression now returned to his usual cool aloofness. "Would you?"

"Yes, I would. To flirt with a colleague could, I understand, be construed as harassment in the workplace. To flirt with a queen could, I'm quite sure, be considered disrespectful at best."

"And at worst?"

She rose and stepped toward him, annoyingly having to tilt her chin upward to meet his direct gaze. "At worst, Xander, it would be considered treasonous."

She held his gaze firm until he laughed. She didn't.

"And, what, Xander do you have so amusing?"

He thrust his hands in his pockets, traces of laughter still lingering on his face as he stepped even closer to her. "You, Ela, you. You are so…" He petered out as he shook his head and his gaze roamed over her face. "So old-fashioned."

"Old-fashioned?" It wasn't what she'd expected him to say, not that she could ever hope to fathom the workings of his mind. "Old-fashioned?" she repeated more loudly.

"Yes! All your talk of treason and respect, it's as if you live in the dark ages!"

She gritted her teeth. "For your information, Xander, I do. My life and that of my people haven't changed for centuries."

"Then you need to change. Really. You need to move into the twenty-first century before you get left behind."

She pursed her lips as she tried to control her anger. "And that, Xander, is exactly what I am trying to do. That is why I'm here, wasting my time trying to talk to you."

"But that's just it, Ela. You're not trying hard enough. You don't even look modern."

"I wear a traditional abaya and hijab and I'm proud of it."

"Of course. I don't mean that. I mean how you hold yourself, as if you have a ramrod stuck up your—"

"You can stop right there!"

He tilted his head to one side. He didn't appear in the least bit fazed. "Ela," he said more gently. "I don't mean to insult you, really I don't. I think you're…" He opened his mouth a few times as if about to say something, before sighing as if he couldn't think of the correct word. "A force to be reckoned with. But, sometimes, you can move mountains more effectively with a little charm, a little softness, a little… *understanding*."

"Understanding," she repeated. He didn't appear to hear the intense, white-hot anger which edged the word.

"Exactly. You need to understand people around you, rather than try to annihilate them."

"And you, Xander, need to stop telling me what to do. It's because of people like you—people who want to command me, people who want to control me, men who wish to bend me to their will, that I have to be what I have become." She hadn't realized her voice had trailed off into barely concealed distress until she saw it reflected in his face. She'd revealed too much. Again.

"I'm sorry, Ela. I truly am. I suspect that it's not you I should suggest be more understanding, but me."

His words reached out to her and connected with her like a life-line, the kind that had never been extended to her before. As the silence between them lengthened, that connection strengthened, too.

He gave a quick shake to his head. "I have no idea what you've been through." He took her trembling hand between his. "But, I promise you this, and"—he smiled ruefully—"no one has asked me to say this. If you wish to educate me, if you wish to tell me anything, anything at all, I'm here for you."

"Why? You obviously don't like me."

His brow furrowed. "That's not true."

"That's how it appears. You even find the idea of flirting with me distasteful."

"I didn't say that. I merely said it was a bad idea. But, believe me, Ela, if we were two ordinary people, I'd flirt with you so hard, that you wouldn't have any option but to fall in love with me."

He took her hand and kissed it. He'd released it before she could remonstrate. But, as she felt its devastating effect travel throughout her body, she thought that maybe, just maybe, she wouldn't have remonstrated at all.

"But we're not," he continued. "So all we can do is to stop antagonizing each other. I'm not so bad, you know. And I know, for sure now, that you are far more complicated than I first thought." His gaze tracked around her face and he traced her cheek lightly with his finger. "Maybe both of us have created masks behind which we can hide. But you know, I suspect you're as beautiful without your mask as you are with it."

She couldn't seem to prevent herself from swaying under the sensory explosion created by his touch to her cheek and to her hand. Her gaze dipped to his lips which opened and, for one long moment, she thought he was about to kiss her. For some reason the thought didn't make her move away. She lifted her eyes to his once more and found his gaze, too, had lowered to her lips. Instinctively she licked them. And then, as if an electric shock had zapped through him he dropped his hands and stepped away. He gave her a quick smile. "I apologize. I got carried away. For a moment I forgot..."

She nodded, not wanting him to finish, not wanting

him to utter the words which were also on her lips. For a moment they'd both forgotten that they hated each other.

Suddenly the sound of a helicopter approaching filled the air with its low thrum. It rapidly brought her back to her senses.

"I have to leave," she said. "I must go," she added, as if she were trying to persuade herself. She backed away and then took half a dozen steps before stopping abruptly. She had to tell him, because he was right. She turned and he was still standing in the same position, watching her. "You're right. We should both drop the masks when we are with each other, because I don't think they're necessary any longer. I think—no, I know—I can trust you."

He nodded. "You can. And I feel I can trust you. We're both new monarchs after all."

"And we're both products of our strange childhoods."

"Damaged orphans thrust into positions of great power. A strange combination."

She smiled and nodded. "And maybe, it's a combination that can only be understood by someone in the same position."

"Indeed."

She nodded, turned and briskly walked away. They were still wary of each other, she knew that, and maybe they'd always be so, but their relationship had shifted from one of combative offense, to one in which they could work together. It wasn't going to be easy, but it would be better.

AND IT HAD BEEN BETTER. Much better than she'd imagined. Over the weeks which had passed since they'd returned to their respective countries, Elaheh had been in daily contact with Xander. And, instead of sparking off each other, they'd worked together to progress their plans. And, more than that, at the end of each video call, they were beginning to share information—personal information.

Elaheh's mind was full of the conversation she'd had with Xander as she switched off the computer screen and allowed her eyes to adjust to the reduced lighting of her bedroom. She sat for a few moments in the dark and remembered how Xander's eyes lit up when he smiled. His lips, she realized now, only ever quirked a little at the corners. The brief movement was gone before you knew it. But the expression in his eyes remained, not only in his eyes, but in the feeling it stirred within her. She frowned as she tried to understand what exactly that feeling was. Warming, was the word she settled on. The heat in his eyes warmed her to her soul... and everywhere else.

She drew in a deep, steadying breath, rose from her chair and wrapped her light robe more closely around her. She walked to the french windows which opened onto a wide balcony a story higher than the lush garden below her window. Her room was at the same level as the tops of the trees and the flowers of the trailing plants whose perfume filled the air. The scent of the flowers, the heat of the night air and the expression in Xander's eyes filled her mind and her body, sending pinpricks of goosebumps over her skin and making her breath somehow hard to catch. Her reaction to him had annoyed her at first. It still did, except now it not only annoyed her but she couldn't stop thinking about it.

She leaned over the balcony's railing and allowed her mind to drift like she never allowed it to do during the day. Xander made her aware of every inch of her body. Her skin tingled as his gaze swept over her, as if he tickled her with a feather, stimulating her skin and sending flutters of sensation through her body to her nerve endings. She flexed her hands as she felt the tingles in her fingers.

Ridiculous. She wanted nothing to undermine her willpower, nothing to make her body needy. She only wanted one thing from men—and that was obedience. The same applied to a husband. She bit her lip when the familiar flutter of panic ran through her at the thought of a husband. She was putting it off, she knew. Despite urgings from her prime vizier, she'd been delaying the matter. The thought of lying with a man scared her to the core. But then she remembered how she felt when Xander looked at her—the flutter in her stomach, the shortness of her breath.

She gripped the rail and mentally shook herself. She needed to get herself out of this ridiculous state of mind. She turned her back on the verdant garden and went back inside her room.

Suddenly she stopped and frowned. Something was different.

"Hello?" she asked tentatively, looking into the shadows. Had someone entered her room? She glanced at the door. It was locked. The key was still there. That left the bathroom. She walked quietly over, opened the door and put on the light. Bright light flooded the room.

She frowned and flicked on the light in her bedroom.

A quick scan revealed no one and nothing out of place. Then why had the fine hairs on her arms lifted? Why did she feel queasy and why were her legs trembling? It was a flight or fight reaction as adrenalin coursed through her veins, triggered by some invisible foe.

Her thoughts tumbled with speed as she went over her movements. She'd only stepped out onto the balcony for a few moments, not long enough for someone to enter the room. And they couldn't besides, because she'd locked it.

She was going crazy. Nothing was different. And yet still she had a prickled sense up her spine that something was wrong. Something had shifted in the room. Her mother used to say that she had a sixth sense about these things. It wasn't something she liked and she'd done her best to ignore it, but now she couldn't.

She sighed and sat on the bed and rubbed her eyes. She put her head in her hands and then she saw it out of the corner of her eye. A piece of paper was neatly folded and placed on her pillow. She froze and the sickly chill returned. It hadn't been there when she'd first entered the room a few hours ago. She'd have noticed because she'd slipped off her watch and placed it beside the bed, beside where the piece of thick cream paper now lay like a serpent, coiled and ready to strike.

If it hadn't been there when she'd entered her room, how had it gotten there?

Her mind raced over what she'd done since she'd retired to her bedroom. She'd been about to shower and undress when the call had come from Xander. She looked at the small alcove where she'd talked with him. She'd have easily seen if someone had entered the room, but the door was locked and no one had passed through it. But...

Her gaze rested on the french windows, still open to the night air. It was always the first thing she did when she entered the room—opened them wide to allow in the air. Hot or cool, she hated being cooped up without fresh air. After opening them, she'd gone directly to the computer where she'd sat, with her back to the open windows.

She licked her lips and walked over to the doors and looked out. Whoever had placed the letter on her pillow must have entered the room from the balcony. She looked around but saw no evidence of entry. Then she looked down the long drop to the garden below but it was too dark to see anything. She went inside, grabbed her phone and switched on the torchlight. With a trembling hand she shone it onto a tree, whose branches reached over the balcony. Immediately she saw a broken branch. Cautiously she took a step closer. The bark had been worn away in two places, as if something of pressure had rubbed against them. She shone the light to the ground, and her fledgling thoughts were confirmed. The under-growth was trampled and there were two clear indenta-tions in the springy grass to show where a ladder had been placed.

Terror filled her. She withdrew immediately and closed the french doors. With fumbling hands she pulled the curtains together and leaned back against them and closed her eyes. Her quarters and the garden lay at the center of a heavily guarded palace. No one could enter it without authority, without being known to the guards. That meant only one thing—whoever had left the message was known to the guards and, most likely, to her. The guards had either allowed the person to enter, or else they'd been dismissed. Either way, she was vulnerable.

With trembling hands she opened the letter.

I will take you to my bed, with or without your consent, because you need me as much as I need you, my love.

It was far more explicit than the other notes she'd received. The trembling in her hands carried on to the rest of her and she had to sit down to fight the weakness and nausea. Someone had been in her room and left a threat to rape her. But not any someone, someone who must be within her elite cadre of officials.

She picked up the phone and a voice answered, asking how they could help. She froze. Was it him? She cleared her throat and said that it was her mistake. She'd be retiring now, and no one was needed.

Who could she trust?

With a start, she turned to the computer. There was only one man who wanted nothing personal from her, which made him trustworthy. Xander wanted nothing from her and he was outside her ring of people she could not trust.

She turned on the radio so no one could hear her and quietly tapped in his contact details, her eyes scanning the room as she typed. It took him a long time to answer and when he did, she didn't recognize him for a moment. Gone were the sharp clothes and western suit, his shirt was half-undone, revealing a chest which was hairier and more muscly than Elaheh had imagined. She was surprised at herself for imagining anything. Then the paper in her hand scrunched, reminding her of why she'd called him.

"Xander," she said her voice hoarse. "I have no one else I can turn to."

.   .   .

Xander listened to Elaheh—her voice hoarse with fear, her face white. He could see her hand was shaking as she shifted her hair away from her face. Two things struck him. One, her hair—it was lustrous and beautiful, and loose. He'd never seen it loose before. If she did take off her hijab, her hair was always pulled back sleekly from her face into a tight knot as if she were scared of letting anything out of her control. It always pulled at her skin which was already tight, making it tighter, and her almond eyes lifted a little at the corners. It was like a mask. But that mask had dropped now and it had an electrifying effect on him.

Then she spoke and her usually firm and clear voice was shaky. He forgot his instant attraction and focused on her panicked eyes.

"What's happened?" he asked, seating himself at the computer, all attention.

She pushed her hair from her face again and poked her head forward to the computer, her eyes large as they searched his. They were all he could see and he saw in them far more of the real Ela than he'd ever seen before. It caused a jolt which created a seismic shift in him. "I..." Her voice caught and so did his heart.

"Take a deep breath," he instructed gently.

To his surprise she did as he said. "Right." She nodded her head, opening her eyes wide as she struggled to take control. "I finished talking to you, went outside briefly, and then came back to my bed, and there was a note there which wasn't there before I spoke to you. Someone had lain a note on my pillow while I was talking to you."

He frowned. "And you're sure it wasn't there before our call?"

She bit her lip and shook her head. "Definitely not. I took off my watch and picked up my robe which lay across the pillow. I would have noticed it then. My sheets are black silk, the note was white."

He was momentarily distracted by the thought of her lying upon black sheets. He hadn't imagined her sleeping against black sheets. It suggested a sensuality which she hid so effectively he'd only suspected it was there. "Okay. So it was placed there when we were on our call."

"I had my back to the bed."

"Was the door locked?"

She nodded. "I always lock it."

"Is there any other way in?"

She glanced anxiously toward the now closed window, and nodded. "The only other way someone could have got in is from the balcony. The doors were open to the night. I'm on the first story, but there are trees and climbers." She glanced at the note she'd dropped on the table in front of her. "Whoever placed the note there, must have climbed in while I was talking to you."

"Is the door locked now?"

She nodded again. "Both doors."

"Right. So, what does the note say?'

He listened as she re-read the note twice. But he didn't need to hear it a second time to understand what was in the mind of the man—for there could be no doubt that it was a man—who wrote it.

"So," she said, after he was silent for a couple of seconds. "What do you think?"

"The same as you, I imagine. If the man who wrote that could enter your room, unseen, then you are in danger and you need to get out of there as soon as possible. Who have you told?"

"No one." She blinked. "Only a few people would be able to enter my chamber. And those few people are the people closest to me. There is no one else I can trust."

"You can trust me." The words escaped his lips before he'd thought them through. But as he played them back in his mind while he registered the shock and relief which showed on her face, he knew he was correct. She *could* trust him. And he was probably the only one.

She nodded. "I know. I thought of you straight away. We may have had our differences, but I feel I can trust you —even, perhaps, *because* of our differences, I feel I can trust you. You are an outsider, with nothing to gain by hurting me."

He winced at the thought of anyone wanting to hurt this woman who was more vulnerable than he'd ever imagined.

"So, I trust you," she continued. "And that's why I called you. Because I don't know what to do. I'm at risk from the very people who are charged with protecting me. And I'm scared. Really scared," she said in a husky undertone which tore at his heart. She didn't need to have added those words because he could see it in her eyes.

"You're probably only at risk from one of those people," he reminded her gently. "But until you know which one, you'll have to treat everyone with suspicion. And," he said, leaning close, echoing her stance, trying to reassure her before he dropped the bombshell, "you'll have to leave. You're not safe there, Ela."

She swallowed and then the unsureness dropped away

and she sat back in her chair, her beautiful lips a straight line of intent. "You're right. But how?"

"Silently, without anyone knowing."

"In disguise?"

"Can you do that?"

She looked at him with a level and fiery gaze. He was relieved to see the stroppy Ela return.

"Of course. I've spent my life in the desert with my people, with only me and my horse. I know how to be ordinary, to fit in, believe it or not."

He didn't, but he had no choice but to give her the benefit of the doubt. "Good. How will you leave?"

She nodded toward the window. "The same way the message was left. Through the window. No one would imagine I'd do that. I can climb down the tree—as a child I always did."

"Is that how you believe the intruder gained access?"

"No. It's not strong enough. I believe he used a ladder. I could see the marks it made. I can use the same tree except I'll drop down into the outer garden."

"Good. Leave quickly, Elaheh. No delays."

"But where shall I go?"

"To me. You'll come to me. And I'll keep you safe until we can work out who is trying to—" He hesitated, not wanting to say the word.

"Rape me," she said coldly. "Rape is control and someone wants to do both to me. And I cannot protect myself physically. All I have to rely on is my mind and that won't protect me from this threat. You're right, I have to leave."

"You said once you're a good horsewoman?"

She nodded. "Of course. I was raised on a horse in the desert."

"Then I suggest you get yourself to the stables, saddle up a horse and ride out toward the mountains, toward me."

"It is too far."

"I'll meet you on your way there."

"There is no village, no oasis, nothing…"

"I will be there."

She opened her mouth to speak but no word came out. But he knew what she was thinking for once, her thoughts were clear in her eyes.

"I promise," he continued. "The important thing is for you to get out of there. You're trapped, a sitting target. Will you come?"

She gave one brief, sharp nod. "I have no choice. I'll change, gather some supplies and water and slip out to the stables and take my horse."

"Can you do it without being seen?"

"I think so. I have no choice but to try."

"Keep on the ancient Bedouin trail toward the mountains and I'll find you in a few hours."

"You'd better be there." It was the last thing she said and he almost chuckled at the return of her assertive self. And for the first time since his instinctive offer to rescue her, he wondered what he was letting himself in for.

CHAPTER 4

Elaheh landed silently in the flower bed. She wiped her hands down her plain black abaya beneath which she wore jeans and a t-shirt—a throwback to when she'd been a teenager. They fitted her still. She stayed only long enough to feel the atmosphere of the garden, to sense if there was anyone else there. It was a still night and her ears strained to pick up the slightest sound which was out of place. There was none. The moon had yet to rise to shed its light inside the courtyard. But it would soon, and then the place would be lit up like daylight. She had to leave before that happened.

Keeping to the path closest to the wall, protected by the trees which edged the garden, she walked quickly to the exit. She was like a shadow merging and drifting into other, darker shadows, until she reached the gate which would take her into yet another garden. The sequence of gardens eventually led to a side door where she could gain access to the stables. The place was deadly quiet. There were no CCTV cameras. Her father had refused to have any such modern intrusion into the palace, and she'd had no reason to believe she needed them. Until now. But there should have been guards. There had always been guards. But not tonight, it would seem. Whoever had placed her note in her room was more powerful than she'd imagined, if he'd had the authority to stand down her guards. Whoever he was, he was powerful, and he wanted her vulnerable. She quickened her pace.

With thudding heart and watchful eyes, she reached the stables. The smell of the place quieted her and she quickly placed a bridle on her horse, nuzzling him and stroking his nose to placate his grumpiness at being awoken. With the reins bunched in one hand she carefully opened the door to the rear exit of the palace. She closed it again and jumped onto her horse, keeping him walking in the shadows before they were sufficient distance to trot away. The trot soon turned into a canter, and then into a full-on gallop as they entered the trail which would take her on a direct route toward the desert castle.

She soon slipped into the rhythm of the rolling gait of her horse and, as the moon rose over the desert, her heart rose with it, despite the danger she was in. This place was her life; it was the desert where she felt most at home, not the palace, not as queen, but as a woman of the land—*her* land. The hijab slipped off her head and her hair flew behind her as she continued on the road to Xander. She dared not imagine him *not* being there because she had no back-up plan.

It wasn't until she'd been riding for an hour and a half that she saw the tell-tale sign of sand rising into the moonlight. At first she was worried it heralded a khamseen wind which would bring fifty days of hot and dusty conditions. But the column of air was contained, narrow, and moving in her direction. It was Xander, she was sure of it. But then doubt filled her mind. What if someone had tracked her down and, instead of following her, had called on someone to head her off?

She galloped behind a clump of thorny trees and bushes and decided to wait to see who it was before making herself known. The quickening breeze hid the hoofmarks of her horse and she slid off him and brought him behind one of the trees from where she would have a good view of the approaching car.

It had no headlights which told her one important thing —it didn't want attention drawn to it. It wasn't until it drew closer and the moon rose higher that she realized it wasn't an ordinary car, but a Land Rover pulling a horse box behind it. She exhaled heavily in relief and slumped against the tree. It must be Xander. Who else would be traveling over the desert with a horsebox? Her people would have followed her by horse and brought her back. But not Xander. She stepped out and flashed her torchlight at him.

He altered his course slightly and pulled up beside her. His window lowered.

"Your Majesty!" he called out, above the sound of the vehicle's engine and her horse's whinny. "I believe you'd like a lift?"

She laughed with relief. "Trust you, Xander," she said, approaching his window. She thought she'd never been so happy to see someone in her whole life.

"I hope you do, Ela," he said, jumping out the vehicle.

"You know what I mean. I thought you'd *ride* out to meet me."

"Me, ride a horse?" he said, unlocking the horse box. "No way. Besides, it's quicker this way. Um, you might like to…" He gestured to her horse, looking uncharacteristically uncertain. Suddenly she understood.

"Don't tell me you don't like horses?"

"I don't like horses."

"Call yourself a desert sheikh?" she said, as she coaxed the horse into the box.

"I don't. I'm sheikh and ruler of my people and I live, very happily, in the city."

He closed the door after she'd made her horse comfortable with food and a drink.

"I don't think we could be more different, you and I," said Elaheh, getting into the Land Rover while he held open the door.

"Maybe," he said, leaning in to pass her the seatbelt. "But fundamentally, Ela, I'm beginning to believe we have the same values. You do trust me, don't you?"

She nodded. She'd been trying to keep brave, trying to respond to his light-hearted conversation, but she couldn't keep it up. "I do," she said in a hoarse whisper. "Now, let's get out of here." She glanced fearfully behind her where she visualized unknown assailants hunting for her, intent on returning her to a man to do whatever he wanted with her.

Xander must have caught her mood because he slammed the door shut, jumped into the Land Rover and turned it around carefully, before driving straight toward the mountains from where he'd come.

She couldn't resist one last look at the haze of lights which indicated her land, her palace, her home. She stifled a sob before it could emerge but not before Xander's quick glance caught it.

"What is it?" he asked, pressing his foot still harder on the accelerator.

She blinked, knowing that it was time for the truth. "When I looked back, I wondered..." She trailed off.

"What?" he pressed.

"I wondered if I'd ever see my country again."

He reached over to her and squeezed her hand. "You will. I promise you, you will. I'll make sure of it."

Unlike before when he'd taken her hand, this time she didn't pull hers away. She needed all his strength and reassurance now.

IT WAS HALF an hour to the mountains and another hour to cover the short route through them. The pass was circuitous, rough and almost impassable. If Xander hadn't been such an expert driver, he thought, he wouldn't have managed to get the horse box through.

"And this, Ela," he said, as they took another horse-shoe bend, below which was a precipitous drop to a deep ravine, "is why we need to get our project started as soon as we can."

Xander didn't know whether it was the moonlight or fear which made Ela's face white. Whatever the reason, the effect on him was to make him protective and angry. Whoever had threatened to rape her was no man. He'd make sure he was found and punished accordingly.

Ela looked down at the steep drop which plunged into an invisible black abyss and then back at him. "I'm certainly not driving back over this pass until the road is improved. By horse, yes. But by car? It's terrifying."

Xander didn't take his eyes off the road. "We're nearly there. And then you'll be safe."

Out of the corner of his eye he saw her sigh, and rest her head against the seat. When he'd first seen her at the oasis, he'd been struck by the fact her hijab had slipped and she was wearing her beautiful dark hair loose, just as she had when she'd spoken to him via video link. She'd lost that rigid, queenly look which was so off-putting and had, instead, simply looked like a beautiful, lost, scared girl, and it pushed all his buttons.

He cleared his throat. He looped around a bend and looked down to the valley below—his land, at last. The border crossing lay immediately around the next bend. He pulled the Land Rover carefully onto the side of the road. "You'd better get into the back with the horse while we cross the border. It's best to leave no trace of your entrance into my country."

She nodded and he helped her into the horsebox. Then he proceeded carefully along the road once more. He pulled up at the first border control which was operated by Elaheh's officials. He lowered his window, and spoke a few words. It only needed to be a few words, given the bribe they'd received on his way here. Obviously supremely grateful for the bribe which easily matched their annual salary, the Tawazun border guards, grinning from ear to ear, indicated he should drive through. He waved and continued on to the next border control—his own this time.

He waved at the guards who saluted and lifted the

barrier. They might well be wondering what their king was doing driving into the night with a horse box, but they made no query and wouldn't spread a word of it. He was their king and they'd happily accepted the same bribe he'd given the Tawazun guards. Nothing earned silence like money, he thought. His mind drifted to Elaheh. She'd have been far too principled to offer money for something she considered should have been done through loyalty. Trouble with Ela, he thought, she was naive. And that was the missing link in her armor; that was what made her vulnerable.

He continued without stopping through his city suburbs, winding his way up to the ridge upon which the palace lay, through quiet city streets along which only a few late party-goers walked. He looked at it through Elaheh's eyes. It would look very different to her traditional country of Tawazun. In that country the only partying going on would be around a campfire, listening to traditional music and stories. He sighed as a dim, distant memory nudged into his mind. One single image —his family. He could see it like a snapshot in his mind— his brother, Roshan, standing hands on hips with the glow of the fire flickering on his face as he made up some story or other for the delight of his parents. His father, slapping his hand on his thigh as he laughed at something Roshan had said. He never saw his mother in his imagination, but he felt her presence all around him because she was holding him. He was seated on her lap looking out, her arms around him, enveloping him in a sense of security and ease for which he'd been searching ever since.

Those memories gave way to later ones, in the same desert oasis with his family, but joined by their most treasured friends. Roshan had several; he had only one. He'd only ever needed one—Selya had been everything to him from the moment he'd met her until the moment his world had come to an end.

He closed down his thoughts immediately. Guillotined them off. He had no place in his life, in his mind, in his heart, for those savage memories. They would break him, and he refused to be broken.

Instead, he frowned with a steely focus, drove into the garage, and pulled on the handbrake with a sense of finality. But the memories, which he'd managed to suppress for so long, lingered. And he knew it had been Ela who had made them surface. For some reason she short-circuited his brain, reached in and tugged at things he tried to forget. He turned off the engine and sighed heavily. And it didn't look like he could avoid her, or how she made him feel. At least, not for the foreseeable future.

He jumped out and looked around. There was no one to witness their arrival. Only his personal guards, and again, they'd been paid to keep their silence. He opened the rear doors and Elaheh, wearing her hijab once more, led her horse down the short ramp and into the stables.

"Go inside. I'll take care of your horse from here," he said.

"Really?" she replied with a smile. He didn't think he'd ever seen her look so natural, despite the tensions of the night.

"Don't look like that," he replied with an ease which was his modus operandi. "I can deal with a horse if necessary." He tugged at the reins and, much to his surprise—and hers—the horse moved and followed him into the stables. He looked behind him. "Don't worry, I've got someone here who will look after her."

"It's a him," she said, with that heart-stopping and all too rare smile of hers.

He glanced at the animal again, noticing immediately what he'd failed to notice before. "Right." Of course it was. A mare wouldn't be fierce enough for Ela to ride. Then he looked back at Ela with even more respect as she walked away.

ELAHEH WAITED IN THE SHADOWS. Despite the ride across the desert, or even because of it, she felt elated. To begin with she had felt sick and scared, but as soon as she'd mounted her horse and started riding cross the desert, it was if shackles had been released from her and she'd felt free for the first time in forever.

And Xander had been there, just as he'd promised. She didn't think she'd ever been so glad to see anybody in her life. The curious thing was that being with Xander was a completely different experience now. The old Xander, the man whose very existence had continually needled her from the first moment she'd met him, had vanished. Now, he was someone who made her feel—she groped for the correct word but could only come up with one— safe.

Through the open door she could see him talking to the stable boy in quiet undertones. He had a natural authority, which had nothing to do with being king. And then he looked up at her and she looked away.

"Ela?" he asked quietly. She didn't trust herself to look around. Then she felt his finger gently touch her chin. There was no force to make her move, but she turned her face toward him and met his gaze anyway. "Come on," he said quietly. "Let's get you inside. It's been a hell of a night."

He extended his hand and she took it and they stepped inside the palace. Unlike hers, his appeared to be full of security cameras which operated the doors, allowing them access deeper and deeper into the building.

They stopped only when they reached an internal garden, distinguishable from the others they'd passed by a more casual air. The plantings were less regimented, the trees and shrubs less severely pruned. Around the small garden were rooms with open windows through which she could see side lights which lit furniture definitely *not* palatial in scale. She looked at him. "These are your private quarters?" She hadn't imagined him in anything less than stark grandeur.

"Yes." He cleared his throat as if he'd been caught out. "This is the oldest part of the palace. Roshan preferred to be located closer to the center of the palace, but I prefer to be here, where my parents lived." He opened a door and followed her inside one of the rooms. "It's full of memories."

She was surprised. Unlike the other parts of the palace through which they'd walked, this had a more homely, comfortable feel about it. She frowned as she noticed the big easy chair in front of a giant TV. It was like some kind of man cave. She looked at him sharply, trying to reassess her vision of him.

"It just seemed easier," he said vaguely.

"Easier?" she asked. "In what way?"

He shrugged. "I guess I mean it's easy for me to relax here. When I'm out there"—he indicated the public part of the palace with a nod of his head—"I'm performing. But in here, I can be myself. I keep it private. Just for myself. Usually," he added with a brief, wry grin.

She looked away, suddenly afraid she was seeing too much of him, the real him. And, more than that, it wasn't the him she thought she knew.

He twisted around and thrust his fingers through his short hair. "Look, I'm afraid if you stay anywhere other than here, where I don't allow anyone to enter, you will be seen, and word will get back."

"Back," she murmured. She turned towards him again. "Back to whom?" she asked. "That is the question. I can't trust anyone, can I?"

He was beside her in an instant. "You can trust me," he said, gripping her arms. She should have thrown off his hands. The old Elaheh would have done. But she knew in the way he gripped her, in the way his fingers pressed lightly but firmly into her flesh, that this was not about control, this was about giving her strength—supporting her, demonstrating that she could rely on him.

She wondered why she had never noticed before how finely drawn his lips were. They weren't full, they normally formed a straight line. But now they were parted softly and her eyes traced their delicate lines. She knew instinctively what they would feel like if they were pressed against hers. She gasped for breath, jerkily struggling to inhale.

"Are you okay, Ela?" he asked anxiously, his frown lowering. "Was the ride too much for you? I know a lot has happened."

She was surprised to feel tears prick her eyes. She couldn't remember the last time someone had held her and expressed sympathy for her situation. She should step away. She opened her mouth to speak but was scared she'd sob, so instead she bit her lip and shook her head again.

For a moment he searched her face, as if trying to work out for himself what she was feeling. And then suddenly he pulled her to him and held her tightly. And in that moment everything changed. She smelled the faint traces of his aftershave, of clean sweat and utter maleness which had never gotten to her like this before. Individually she'd registered them, but when combined they held a force which she had no idea if she could resist.

She pressed her hands against his chest with the intention of pushing him away but she didn't. Instead, her fingers splayed over the fine cotton of his shirt, registering the muscles and hard chest beneath. Without thinking, she pressed her cheek to his chest. The hairs tickled her cheek and when she moved they stimulated her skin. She could hear and feel the thud of his heart through her ear and through her body. It was as if they had become one, merged by the pulse of his blood pumping through his veins and the contact of his skin against hers.

His heartbeat quickened as, instead of taking her hands away, she glided them over his chest, her fingertips searching out the undulating sinews and muscles which shifted under her touch.

"What are you doing, Ela?" he asked, his voice rumbling into her ear, melding with his heartbeat, making her feel him in a way she'd never felt another person before.

She shifted her head so her forehead was pressed against his bare chest and her eyelashes flickered against his skin. She was only a breath away from kissing the bare patch revealed by his open shirt. There was no thought that entered her mind as she pressed her lips against his bare flesh.

Suddenly his hands were around her head, forcing her to look up at him. His dark eyes flared with surprise, and something else, something more dangerous. For a long moment she didn't know if he was going to kiss her or shout at her. To her biting disappointment the desire in his eyes faded and his eyes grew harder.

"Ela! What the hell do you think you're doing?"

She swallowed. "I… I wanted to kiss you."

"Kiss me?" he repeated, shaking his head.

"I've never kissed a man before, you see. Never been held tenderly by a man." A look that she'd have described as disappointment flickered across his features. This was Xander, she reminded herself. She cleared her throat. "I simply wanted to know what it was like."

His grunt of surprise traveled through her body, in the same way his heartbeat did, filling her with himself, and creating patterns of feeling in her body which were entirely new.

"And what was it like?" His voice was a shade lower now.

She looked up at him. "It was … nice."

"And do you know what else is nice?" She shook her head. "A kiss on the lips," he continued. "Would you like to try that?"

She was mute. She couldn't conjure up any words, even if she wanted to. And words were the last thing on her mind at that moment. She nodded. There was no other honest answer she could give.

His beautiful lips, quirking lightly at the corner, was the last thing she saw before they pressed to hers, and everything changed. The first thing she felt was a devastating, but not unwelcome, invasion of her privacy as the heat of his breath and his lips enveloped hers. To begin with their touch was tentative, but as she suddenly found her hands had slid around to his back, bringing him closer to her, the kiss became more intense. She felt him groan into her mouth which immediately sparked a feeling inside of her which threatened to derail her senses.

She could hear quickened breathing and was vaguely surprised to realize that it was her own. His hands were tight around her now too, and when she felt his tongue touch hers her response went off the scale. She pressed her body against his, in a purely intuitive, purely animal, reaction. All she knew was that she needed that hard chest pressed against her, those arms wrapped around her, so she could become one with him. She found herself doing things she didn't know she could do, and didn't know she wanted to do, rising against him. She felt a growing hardness press into her stomach.

Eventually he pulled away, dragging himself as if he'd been drugged and the sluggish chemical was fighting his willpower. "Ela!" He swore softly under his breath.

Once more, she raised herself on tiptoes to try to encourage him to kiss her again. But he made no movement to claim her lips again. She put her hands behind his head and pulled him to her, trying to command, trying to use all her willpower to get what she wanted from this stubborn man. But still he did not yield.

"Kiss me again, Xander, I *want* you to kiss me again."

"No, Ela, it's not possible."

She shook her head. "You're wrong, it *is* possible, of course it is, you just kissed me. I want you to kiss me like that again."

"That," he said, sweeping his thumbs over her cheeks as he held her face between his hands, "is not a good idea. I kissed you once because you've never been kissed."

She felt shocked and deflated. "You only kissed me because you felt sorry for me?"

Again that slight quirk of the lips. "No way, Ela. I kissed you because I wanted to, and also because I wanted you to know what it was like. One kiss is one thing, the second kiss is an entirely different matter."

"Maybe I want that different matter."

"And so, maybe, do I. But it's not going to happen. You are here because you trust me. And pretty soon you will cease to trust me if I kiss you again."

She shook her head. She couldn't imagine not trusting him. "I *want* you to kiss me." She could hear her imperious tone returning, and she didn't like it.

He reacted instantly to it, and stepped away. His hands gripped her shoulders as before, but this time he didn't do it to make her trust him, he did it to hold her away from him.

"I repeat, Ela," he said, "this is not going to happen. Now, let me show you where you are going to sleep." He led her to a bedroom that was obviously personal, obviously male. She looked up at him as the confusion of lust slowly faded and comprehension dawned. "But this is your room, surely?"

He released her and stepped away. "It's yours now, for as long as you want it." He indicated an interconnecting door. "I'll sleep in the dressing room for now. Nobody comes to these rooms unless I ask them to." He gave a small smile. "They will simply assume I'm reverting to the slobbish student ways I had as a boy. You are safe here, Ela. You are safe from others and you are safe with me."

"But you didn't kiss me again as I asked." She couldn't bear to look him in the eye any more to see his derision.

"Ela, don't you understand? I couldn't trust myself. One thing could lead to another and your virginity isn't a thing to be taken lightly."

His words were like an icy dousing of cold water on a hot day. She gasped as the shock blew away the last remaining traces of arousal, and confronted her head-on with her reality. She felt a blast of anger—at her past, at what had happened to her and at Xander's assumption.

"I am not a virgin, Xander. Not. A. Virgin." She practically spat out the last words through rigid lips, which had forgotten the kiss.

His eyes widened with shock and, she realized, understanding. "And, yet, you say you've never kissed anyone."

She was silent in horror. She'd allowed her anger to overwhelm her and to reveal her secret, her inner shame. She swallowed and shook her head, as her mind raced to try to withdraw the words she'd uttered, to form words which would erase them.

"I..." She felt tears spring to her eyes. She swiped at them and twisted away from him. She couldn't let him see. "I... I'm tired," she whispered in a croaky voice.

He was silent for a few moments, waiting for her to speak, but she couldn't. There were only the dots to be connected to form a truth which she refused to voice.

Even when she felt his light touch on her arm, she refused to turn to him.

"Please, go," she said, her flaming and tear-soaked face twisted away from him.

She heard him leave and close the door behind him.

She was alone once more. Just as she always was. Except now, after the closeness she had felt only minutes earlier, she felt more alone than ever; after the near revelation of a shame about which few people knew, she felt more vulnerable than ever.

Without undressing, she climbed into bed and curled up into a ball and cried as she should have cried years earlier.

XANDER CLOSED the door quietly behind him and walked across to the drinks cabinet. He poured himself a generous whiskey, frowned into its amber depth briefly, before knocking it back, and placing the empty glass firmly back onto the table. He needed that potent heat to counter the fire in his heart which her words had ignited.

He twisted around and looked out the window, over the lights of his city, toward the mountain range which marked the divide between his country and Ela's, with only one thought on his mind.

What the hell had happened to Ela, that she was no longer a virgin, and yet she'd never been held tenderly by a man, had never been kissed? Because he didn't doubt the veracity of her statements. One sure thing he knew about Ela was that she never lied. Which left a question, the answer to which he couldn't bear to contemplate.

"You have no choice, Xander," confirmed Zavian. "We are all in agreement. Elaheh must continue to stay with you. The chances of detection are greater if she moves and, besides, no one will suspect her of being with you, given your obvious and public antipathy toward each other."

Xander glared at the computer screen which was split into four—himself, one each for Amir and Zavian and the last shared by Roshan and Shakira.

"It's impossible," Xander said.

Shakira leaned forward. "In what way?"

Xander mind was filled with the memory of the hurt and vulnerability he'd seen in Elaheh's face, and the lingering question which had stopped him from sleeping —how had she lost her virginity without a single kiss or tender caress? Bile rose in his gut and he could feel rage rising at the thought. His rage must have registered on his face because when he turned back to the cameras, Roshan was shaking his head and the others looked concerned. But it was Shakira who spoke first.

"Xander, you have to try to ignore her outbursts." Xander grunted softly under his breath, aware that Shakira and the others had misinterpreted his response. "Beneath that demanding, imperious facade is a woman who needs your help."

He pressed his fingers against his closed eyes, trying to force the anger to retreat. It didn't. He looked at each of the kings in turn before letting his gaze rest on Shakira. For a moment he considered telling them what he suspected. Or, at least, telling Shakira. But what could he tell them? Nothing for sure. He only had suspicions, for now at least. But he vowed he'd discover the truth, and the only way to do that was to continue to protect her. "I know," he said finally. "I've cleared the next seven days of all engagements and meetings."

"Good." Shakira sat back in her seat, her beautiful face showing relief. Not for the first time Xander wondered what would have happened if he'd stayed the night of the masquerade ball. Whether he'd stood a chance with the mysterious, beautiful Shakira. Somehow he doubted it. And he was glad, because instead he'd gained a friend and a beloved sister-in-law.

"I know you don't particularly like Elaheh," said Amir. "But you *will* need to keep her close until we know who is behind these threats. Xander, you can't let her out of your sight."

"Amir, I may be many of the things people say about me, but one thing I'm not is dishonorable. I will keep Elaheh safe because I'm unable to do anything else. But"— he leaned into the camera, eyeballing each of them in turn, needing to return to the Xander they knew and understood, because it was the only Xander *he* knew and understood—"when I go mad, I want you to take responsibility!"

The lighter tone broke the ice and they grinned back at him in relief. He sighed, switched off the computer and jumped up. He had to get away. And he knew precisely where to go—the only place where he could achieve a sense of peace, where nobody could get to him. He swam alone on a private beach daily, usually in the early morning, but this morning his swim had been delayed by the conference call. Sometimes he thought the daily swim was the one thing which kept him sane.

He took only the bare essentials but hadn't gotten as far as the door when he heard his name called through the interconnecting door which led to the bedroom in which Elaheh was sleeping. He stopped in his tracks at the sound of Elaheh's voice. It was a beautiful voice, deep for such a slight woman, and more inviting than she appeared in person. It got to him, just as that glimpse of the real, vulnerable woman had got to him the previous night. A part of him wanted to move on, wanted to return to the routine he knew, but a bigger part of him couldn't turn away from that voice.

He knocked on the door and she immediately opened it, as if she'd been waiting. The first thing he noticed was that she wasn't wearing a hijab to cover her hair. Her mane of dark hair was still pulled off her face but in a softer style. Presumably she wasn't accustomed to doing her own hair, because there was something endearingly messy about it which further loosened the screw inside him, softening him even more toward her.

"Ela." The nickname slipped out before he could stop it. But this time he didn't see a corresponding frown lower on her face. She looked concerned, and vulnerable. He remembered Shakira's words. This woman needed his help—nothing more, nothing less. "You're not wearing your hijab. Is everything okay?"

She pressed her lips together and gave a brief smile. "As well as it can be, considering I'm in hiding."

He gave her an answering smile. "Hopefully it won't be for long."

"Indeed." Her chin tilted at a determined angle, but the smile still lingered on her lips. "I'm not wearing my hijab because I had a video call with my advisors. I wanted them to be able to see me clearly, to see that I was well. Thank you, by the way for setting up the computer for me."

"You're welcome. If the technician wondered why I wanted it set up without any possibility of being traced, he didn't ask."

Her smile warmed. "You are king, after all. Your command should be followed without question."

"True. Although I think it will take me some time to get used to it. So how did the call go? Did you satisfy them?"

"I think so. It's about that I wish to talk to you."

"What is it, Ela?" he asked, his voice gentler now.

She plucked at her abaya with uncharacteristic unsureness. The smile had slipped away now, vanished into doubt and uncertainty.

"Has something happened?" he pressed.

"My vizier asked me to tell him where I am. He says that he needs to know for security reasons." She looked at him with those beautiful feline eyes which curved up in a way which never failed to turn him on. Even when she'd infuriated him, he'd had to fight an equally strong arousal.

He frowned. "Did you tell him?"

"No. But I wanted to. I've grown up with the man. He knows everything about me. Surely it wouldn't hurt to reassure him. He says he's terribly worried about me."

"Don't tell him."

"But I have to tell someone, some time. I can't stay here forever."

"Don't tell him," he repeated. "Until we find the person who sent you that letter it's not safe to tell anyone."

"Okay," she said, in a surprisingly meek tone. It hurt him to see her diminished and living in fear. He almost wished to see her imperious attitude return. Almost. She looked down at the towel he held. "Are you going somewhere?" Her tone was as wistful as her expression. He hadn't seen her eyes quite so vulnerable before. Shakira's advice repeated in his brain.

"Yes." He paused but couldn't bring himself to walk away from her. "Would you care to join me?"

Her face lit up and his heart sank. "That would be lovely. I can't bear the thought of being cooped up here a moment longer. Where are you going? To the mountains?"

He frowned. "Why would I go to the mountains?"

The light in her face faded a little. She shrugged. "It's where I always head when I want time out."

"Why?" He was quite perplexed at the thought.

"Because it's quiet and beautiful and it's my place. But... you're not going there."

He shook his head. "No, I'm going to the beach. I swim every morning." It was her turn to look perplexed.

"Why?" she asked.

"Because," he said firmly, "it's quiet and beautiful and it's my place."

There was a pause before they both burst out laughing at the same time. It was Ela who spoke first.

"You and I are opposites, aren't we?"

"In some way, most definitely. But you're still welcome to join me if you can put up with the beach."

"I'd like that. And then, maybe, when it's safe, we can go to the mountains."

It would have been churlish of him to refuse, and the look in her eyes definitely didn't make him want to.

"Of course. And *I'd* like that." He didn't know why he added that. The words emerged out of some deep impulse. "Come on then."

"Are you sure it's safe?"

"Absolutely. It's private. No staff, no public, only the royal family and their most honored guests have access to these rooms, and the path to the beach."

"Right." She nodded and gave him a half-hearted smile. Her unsureness rattled him. "Right," she repeated, trying to sound more confident. It didn't work.

He opened the door. "This way."

She halted in the impressive vaulted hall, as he knew she would. They were surrounded on all sides by decorative tiles and columns and gilded portraits of previous royalty, which she wouldn't have seen in the darkness of the previous night. They exchanged glances. "This is beautiful," she said, arching her neck to look up to where the morning light streamed through the clerestory windows. "And cool."

He pointed upward. "It's the latticed air vents. They allow the sea breeze to enter the corridors and rooms. Makes it more comfortable all year round."

She took a deep breath. "And it smells beautiful, too," she said, as they continued walking.

"The gardens were established centuries ago and well tended. Is it so very different to your own palace?"

She smiled and raised an eyebrow. "You've never been there, have you?"

He shook his head. "No, I've not had the pleasure." Not that he'd thought of it in those terms before.

She stopped by a large pot overflowing with crimson fluted flowers. She fingered the velvety petals of a blossom. "Yes, it's very different. The harshness of the climate in my country, and the toughness of my people, is reflected in the buildings. My palace is much older and..." She hesitated as she looked around, as if groping for the correct word. Then she turned to him, bringing the blossom to her nose to inhale its fragrance. "And less decorative, you could say." Xander guessed you could. He'd heard her palace looked like a prison. "We also can't grow tender exotic blossoms such as these," she continued, looking up at him with a guilty look. "But, of course, there are many other qualities about it which are magnificent."

"Of course." He just couldn't think of any. And nor, it seemed, could she.

She glanced around the paintings and stopped at one. She looked at Xander. "Who's this?"

He didn't need to look to know. "My great grand-mother. She was a beauty."

She turned too quickly and caught him looking at *her*, not the portrait. His great grandmother had been a great beauty but it was Ela's own beauty which he couldn't help admiring. She blushed before turning quickly away again.

"I was just thinking she looked like you," Ela said.

"Does that make her more of a beauty or less?" asked Xander, enjoying toying with this more vulnerable version of Ela.

She raised an eyebrow and a small smile played on her lips. "Fishing for compliments?" she asked.

He took a step closer. "It's nice to think of yourself as being admired by someone you like."

Her smile dropped but the air of vulnerability didn't.

"You like me." There was a sense of wonder in her voice which surprised him.

"That wasn't even a question, was it?"

She shrugged. "I'm surprised, that's all. After all the arguments we've had, after all the disagreements. I'm surprised to know you like me."

"Then it will really surprise you to know that I've always liked you."

"Then why were you so antagonistic towards me?"

"Me, antagonistic? That's rich. You made it quite plain that you had no time for me. What was it you once called me, 'a dilettante, arrogant playboy'?"

"Well you are. Or, at least, you were."

His lips tweaked with amusement again. "So you don't consider me to be so any longer."

Confusion flickered over her beautiful face.

"What is it?" he asked, taking another step towards her.

She held out her hand to stop him. "Don't."

"Don't what?"

"Come so close." She shrugged. "I can cope with you being close and not speaking, and I can cope with difficult questions if you aren't close. But I can't cope with both at the same time."

The thought that he could disrupt her unflappable confidence sent his libido into overdrive. But he needed to focus, not seduce. "Then I'll step away, because I'd really like an answer to my question."

She pressed her palm to her chest as if trying to calm herself. He liked that, too. "What was the question?"

He grinned. "It wasn't really a question. More an intrigued statement. I was surprised that you no longer think of me as an arrogant playboy. I guess I wanted to hear you say it again."

She pressed her lips together as if unsure how to reply. After a few long seconds which he was determined not to interrupt, she smiled and stepped toward him, apparently having overcome her unsureness. "You, Xander, are needy. And no, I will not elaborate on that statement. You'll have to make of it what you will."

He grinned and shook his head in despair. The old Elaheh had just resurfaced. She was an enigma. One moment terrifying, the next as vulnerable as hell. In a flash he thought that in both states she was utterly mesmerizing. He turned away suddenly. What he needed was a good, long, cooling swim.

He sighed heavily and followed her out to the garden.

· · ·

ELAHEH WAS RELIEVED to find that Xander was correct and the path to the beach was, indeed, short and totally private. The footpath gave way to a small, sheltered cove which was fringed by trees and protected from the city by a rocky promontory.

As soon as Xander set foot on the sand he tilted his head up to the sun, closed his eyes and sighed.

"That feels good," he said. "Are you coming into the water?"

"No, thank you. I don't like to swim. I'll sit in the shade."

He began to take off his clothes and Elaheh looked quickly away and walked toward some chairs and tables placed under the shade of large palm trees. Beside it a thatched bar stood, no doubt stocked with everything from the ubiquitous champagne to whatever else a royal might need to relax.

"Help yourself to a drink," he called out.

She opened the drinks cooler, allowing the chill air to fan her heated skin for a few seconds before glancing over the top of the bar to where he was undressing. She couldn't take her eyes off him. As he stripped off his shirt, she was aware of only one thing—the way his muscles bunched and stretched as he raised and lowered his arms. His dark skin gleamed with a slick of sweat which made her mouth water. The thought was alarming, but didn't stop her from thinking about him. Sunshine and shadows highlighted the contours of his shoulders. She was glad he had his back turned to her. She could watch him unobserved. Standing in his swimming shorts she could admire his muscled legs—runner's legs, she thought idly. Not that she'd ever seen any man's legs before, running or walking. But if she had, she knew they'd be like that.

He ran into the sea and dived into the water. She could almost feel the chill of the water hitting his heated skin. She shivered as he swam strongly out into the sea. She watched until her eyes hurt and he was a dot in the distance.

With a sigh she closed the cooler and opened a can of soda. She'd hardly slept the previous night and suddenly felt exhausted. The tension which had kept her going all morning suddenly dissolved under the sound of the rhythmic roll and drag of the ocean on the sandy beach. She lay on the sun lounger, closed her eyes to the flicker of shadows created by the rattling fronds of the palm trees, and lost herself to dreams of Xander, as sleep crept over her like a soft, light comforter.

XANDER LOOKED DOWN at Ela with a frown. She lay, fast asleep, on the sun lounger, sheltered from the sun by the dancing fronds of a palm tree. She looked peaceful in a way she never did when she was awake. She also looked young and intensely vulnerable. He hated that because he knew it brought out the best in him. And the best of him would make his life very difficult.

He reached for his towel and began to dry himself with his back to her. He didn't want her to think he'd been looking at her. He plucked a bottle of soda water from the fridge and lay on a lounger next to her. The mid-morning sea breezes were picking up and the palm leaves were dipping and swaying above their heads. As he sipped his drink and gazed determinedly out to sea, and occasionally to Ela, he couldn't stop himself from thinking and feeling a million things he'd never allowed himself to feel before.

By the time she awoke, and turned to look at him, the clouds of sleep still lingering in her eyes, he knew that he was doing more than look out for her—he was falling for her and he wasn't sure he'd be able to pull himself out from under her spell.

"I've been asleep," she said surprised, sitting up. "I never sleep during the day."

"Maybe your sleep at night has been disturbed."

"It always is. I'm simply a bad sleeper."

"Not just then you weren't," he said, handing her a drink.

"It's strange," she said, her relaxed mood still prevailing. "There's something about this place which makes me feel..." She frowned. "Calm and..."

"Safe," he prompted. She turned to him and nodded.

"I can't remember the last time I felt like this."

"That's good." He didn't add that it made him feel good that he could protect her, that he could make her feel safe. He didn't think she'd appreciate that knowledge. Not yet, anyway.

"Is it?" Her beautiful brow furrowed. "Shouldn't I feel safe and calm in my own land?"

He nodded slowly. "You should, and you will. Once you've got this out the way."

"Even before this I always felt... on guard."

He remembered Shakira's words. "Defensive."

"Yes, I've had to be."

Instinctively he reached out and placed his hand on her arm. She lifted her head sharply. "You don't need to defend yourself against anyone here, or anyone in the future. I'll make sure of that. There will be no one who will attack you."

"How can you be so certain?"

"Because I'll make sure of it."

She smiled. "Thank you. I can't see *how* you'll make sure of it, but I appreciate the sentiment."

She swung her legs off the recliner and he caught a glimpse of slim ankles and narrow feet as her abaya lifted briefly. Their delicacy got to him. He looked up to find her watching him. She rose and twitched her abaya back to cover her legs.

He stood up and determinedly looked away, out to the navy blue line of the horizon. He narrowed his gaze as if looking at something in particular. But the only thing he was doing was thinking of some*one* in particular—the woman who stood, uncertain, by his side.

They both began to speak at the same time.

Xander thrust his fingers through his short hair. "You go first."

"No, please you."

"I just wanted to apologize, Ela. I should never have kissed you last night."

She narrowed those beautiful eyes on him. "And why is that?"

He shrugged. How could he put his thoughts into words? "It was an impulse, and not one I should have indulged. I'm sorry."

Her face turned pale and impassive, devoid of emotion. She grunted and gave a slight, measured shrug. "It's not important."

It was his turn to feel the emotion turn to chill. He felt

the reverse. He'd apologized because it *had* felt important. And to hear from her that it meant nothing made him feel an idiot.

Her mouth was firm and her lips pursed as she smoothed down her abaya, looking everywhere but at him. Her actions reinforced the fact that he was of no more importance to her other than someone to guard her in this one moment of need. And he knew that as soon as that need was over, she'd be gone.

"It's time we returned," she said crisply. "There may be news."

"Sure," he said. "As well as my inquiries, the other kings and Shakira are also looking into it."

"Good. Then I'm sure I won't have to be your unwanted guest for much longer."

She turned on her heel and walked across the beach toward the path. And all he could do was follow her and muse on the thought that it hadn't taken her long to return to her old, cold ways.

He was falling for her and he didn't want to be. He'd contact Roshan and the others and let them know that she definitely couldn't stay here any longer. She had to go. But, even while he was thinking this, he knew that he would only let her go if she was safe. They might have no future together, but it didn't make him stop caring for her.

ELAHEH WALKED SWIFTLY along the track toward the palace. She couldn't bear to look at him in case her outward cool crumpled, and he realized the truth—that she'd lied to him. She'd told him his kiss wasn't important, and it was. Because his kiss had made her aware that she wanted him like she'd never wanted a man before. Because for the first time in forever she thought of a man without fear, and without distaste.

But she'd been wrong. She'd been tricked by the kiss into almost believing that she could have what so many women the world over had—the love of a good man—both physical and emotional. And she couldn't. Because even if Xander had any interest in her—and it certainly didn't sound as if he did—that interest would swiftly disappear once he knew the truth about her.

CHAPTER 6

The next day Elaheh awoke to the muezzin's call to prayer coming from the city's great mosque. The cooler air of the sea breeze caressed her bare skin, and she felt an unusual sense of peace. Then she suddenly remembered where she was. *Not* her country. *Not* her palace. A rap at the door sent her reaching for her bedclothes, and realizing that it had been the sound that had awoken her from her deep sleep. She sat up with a start.

She slid down the bed. "Come!"

Xander opened the door slowly and looked in warily. He looked away sharply. "I'm sorry," he said, staring at the door, "I didn't think you'd still be in bed. I'll come back later."

"Have you found anything?" she asked.

He paused, part way closing the door, his hand gripping the door handle like a lifeline. "No," he said, his eyes still firmly turned away from her. "Unfortunately not. Our investigations haven't turned up anything. But we do have a lead on the notepaper used, and we're following that up."

"The notepaper?"

"Yes, he made the mistake of using a hallmarked paper which originated from only one manufacturer. I have someone in Paris checking out the retailers who stock it. Of course, online sales will be difficult to trace. But not impossible."

She nodded slowly, her mind racing to try to remember if she knew anyone who'd returned from Paris in the past year. "You forget, my country doesn't do much in online sales." She looked at him, frozen in the door way, talking to the door. "Xander! Come on in. I hardly think we need to stand on ceremony with everything that's happening!"

"Right," he said closing the door and stepping into the room, his eyes apparently now transfixed by the view outside the window. "Right," he said as if trying to persuade himself that it truly was right.

She grunted with impatience. "Stay there, and I'll put on my robe."

As he turned his back to her, she leaped out of bed and grabbed a robe, tying it firmly around her. "You can turn around now."

But when he turned she blushed, as the expression in his eyes wasn't as business-like as she'd anticipated.

She cleared her throat, and forced her hands away from the knotted sash which was the only thing hiding her nakedness. She met his eyes steadily. "As I said, online shopping isn't big in my country.

"That makes it easier. Hopefully we'll have news soon.

But, in the meantime." He pressed his lips together as if reluctant to speak.

"In the meantime?" she prompted. "What? You want me to leave?"

"Yes. Having you here, is proving… difficult."

"For whom? You're the only one who knows I'm here."

He nodded. "For me. Our relationship has never been easy and, I fear…" He trailed off, as if at a loss for words. He was never at a loss for words.

She held up her hand as if to stop a flow of words which had already stopped. He obviously deeply regretted their brief kiss. It made her angry, because she couldn't regret it. "That's fine. You needn't say anything further. Your meaning is quite clear. You want me to leave, and I shall."

He sighed and put his hands on his hips, her anger breaking down his last remaining shreds of discomfort. "Don't do that, Ela!"

"Do what?"

"Go all queenly on me. Jump to conclusions."

"I thought you'd be pleased I agree to your demands. I thought it would make life easier for you."

"Nothing to do with you will make my life easy." They stared at each other in impasse. It was Xander who broke the silence. "Look, I didn't mean that. What I want is for you to listen to me. I'm not telling you to leave me. I'm saying that we should both leave here together. I've spoken to Roshan and he's suggested we move to the desert palace where the kings meet. We'll be less… on top of each other there. There will be more physical space and, I believe you'll be more comfortable in the desert."

She tilted her head to one side. "And you're coming with me?"

He nodded his head. "It's been agreed."

She suddenly understood. "The others have persuaded you to go with me."

He gave one brief nod, and in that she understood everything. He couldn't wait to get rid of her. A jab of pain filled her, swiftly followed by an unfamiliar emotion she refused to name. She quashed it as quickly as it had risen.

"I hadn't realized you disliked me so much. When you kissed me, it didn't seem like it." The moment the words had tumbled out she regretted them.

"Ela! You have to understand! I don't dislike you and I enjoyed our kiss—I did," he added. She didn't know if he were trying to persuade himself or her. "But that is exactly what makes this whole situation impossible! You're vulnerable and I have no intention of taking advantage of that vulnerability. And, to be honest, I'm afraid that things could get out of hand. On a personal basis," he said, his vagueness hiding nothing.

She exhaled a tightly held breath of understanding. "Ah. You can rest assured that nothing will get out of hand. I'm not keen for my future to include a man."

"And why is that?" There was nothing about the tone of his question that was casual. It was evident in the tone, and in his eyes, and the way he stopped shifting around and stood, motionless, awaiting her reply.

"A man will bring me no joy, and I certainly won't be able to make a man happy."

"And why is that?" he repeated. It seemed he was determined to get to the root of her pain.

They stared at each other in stony impasse for a few moments, as the secret she kept tight inside her began to ache, as if it wanted to find the relief of openness. She drew in a breath as if about to speak but shook her head instead.

"And why is that?" Xander repeated once more. Then he stepped towards her and she knew that her secret was in danger, as the protective shell with which she'd so competently surrounded herself began to fracture. The thudding of her heart grew louder. It filled her body, her ears, her head. She thought she'd burst as the thudding grew in intensity. She couldn't seem to get her breath.

"Ela?" Xander repeated. "Are you okay?"

She couldn't speak. If she did, she thought her heart would literally jump out of her mouth. Either that or a scream would emerge. And she instinctively knew that that scream wouldn't be a ladylike sound of alarm, but would have all the primeval intensity of an animal cornered.

Then Xander did something she wished he hadn't—he reached out tentatively toward her. She just stared at his hand and then back at him, and he withdrew his hand to his side.

But still she felt unable to move, consumed by the beating of her heart and the mounting panic which had risen from someplace deep inside of her. It reminded her of the time and place when she had felt the same. After that she had buried it tight, encased it in solid scar tissue, and embalmed it so that it was watertight, emotion-tight, invulnerable. But now, somehow, after all these years, this man before her had cracked its shiny hard surface with one slight tap of his hand and a split had occurred, which had let out that thing which lay inside of her.

"Ela? You have to tell me what's going on." He stood with his hands on his hips, anxiety etched in his expression. His eyes darted around her face before sighing heavily. "I'm not going anywhere until you tell me what's going on." He reached out again and this time nothing she could say or do would make him stop. He put his hands firmly around her shoulders and dipped his head and stared into her eyes. "Whatever it is you're hiding, you need to tell me."

She tried to pull his hands away but they wouldn't move; she tried to claw his fingers, prize them from her flesh but they only dug in deeper.

"You can't push me away this time, Ela. It's time to tell me what the hell is going on inside that beautiful head of yours. Tell me what happened to you, tell me what has made you so scared of men. Tell me," he repeated.

Terrified, she pressed her lips together and shook her head, tight little shakes, but the pounding of her heart only increased. She began to feel dizzy, as the world moved, shifted, as if it were torn down the middle, stopped making sense. The tears which had misted her eyes gathered and trickled down her cheeks. She was shaking now. Her lips were trembling with the effort of keeping her mouth closed. Then she could do it no longer and she closed her eyes tight, hoping that still she might be able to control the raging torrent of emotion which threatened to consume her.

He brought her to him and held her tight. It was as if the wave of emotion transferred to him, relieving her of the pressure. She might not have told him her secret, but, somehow he'd lessened her pain.

Eventually he pulled away and held her shoulders gently, his eyes searching hers. "Ela, whatever is going on, please tell me." His voice was gentle now, too. It was time.

She bit her lip and nodded. "Everyone wishes me to marry. But…"

"Go on," he urged.

"I'm scared. Marriage. I'm scared of it because there is no way I can make any man happy." She turned to him, her cheeks blazing like a beacon, and her eyes bright with tears.

He frowned and cocked his head to one side. "What are you talking about? Of course you can. You are beautiful, intelligent and"—he sighed—"sexy as hell. So I don't see why you think you cannot make a man happy."

She hadn't wanted to tell anyone how she felt. It was her secret, locked up inside of her alongside all the other trauma she'd suffered. Sealed with a kick.

"Just take it from me, I can't."

"No, I won't take anything except the truth. How can I understand if you don't tell me?"

"Understanding isn't required. Marriage isn't for me, and that's that."

"I'm not leaving until you give me a proper answer. Tell me why you have no wish to marry."

She frowned at his insistence. Why did he care whether or not she married? It wasn't as if this was anything personal for him, was it?

"Please, Ela. Tell me what you're so afraid of."

She licked her lips. "Relations, between a man and a

woman." His frown deepened. "For heaven's sake, Xander, I'm afraid of sex. Something happened, you see, and I can't bear the thought of it."

His hands froze on her shoulders, just as his eyes froze over hers. She felt the change in him like she knew she would. She'd hoped he'd understand, or at the very least accept her for what she was about to tell him. But she knew, deep in her heart that he wouldn't. He was a man after all. And men didn't like used goods, didn't care for unpleasantness.

"What happened?" he asked, his voice hoarse with emotion. This time she didn't fight him, lifting her chin so she faced him. Suddenly all the fight had left her.

"I was raped. I was young…" She swallowed. "It was a stranger. A Bedouin nomad. Mad, I think. He took me away, did what he did, and then dumped me back at the camp."

She watched as Xander swallowed a lump. She kept her eyes on his throat as it convulsed. It was easier than seeing the inevitable disgust and pity in his eyes.

"Did your father know?" he asked eventually.

"He never knew. My mother kept it secret, made up a story to cover my hospital visits." He didn't speak and she suddenly realized that the noise of the thumping of her heart had stopped, and she was filled with an unexpected sense of peace. The worst had happened. Her shameful secret was out. She sighed and lifted her eyes to his. She blinked as she tried to reconcile her expectations with the sight of Xander in tears.

They weren't just a glazing in the eye but tears rolled down his face and his eyes… the expression within them revealed a depth of hurt and agony, the like of which she wouldn't have dreamed lay inside of Xander.

She cupped his cheek with her palm. "Xander! I'm sorry."

"Sorry?" He did nothing to wipe away his tears but, instead, held her tight. He pressed his cheek to the top of her head. She could feel the damp of his tears penetrate her hair. *She* didn't cry. She didn't think she'd ever cry again. "What are you sorry for?"

"For having your opinion of me changed. I can't bear the thought of sex, I never intend to have sex. I can never make a man happy, and I can never be made happy by a man. It's that simple."

"There's nothing simple about this." He swore under his breath and held her face tight in his hands. "Listen to me, Ela. You're wrong. Something awful was done to you and it wasn't your fault. It resulted in damage, which also wasn't your fault. And your fear of sex, that, also is not your fault. You can't keep punishing yourself for something which wasn't your fault."

"I'm simply stating the facts."

"Okay, I accept they are facts as you see them now. But I want you to promise me something."

"What?"

"I want you to give me a chance, to show you what love can be like between a man and a woman."

"You've been so good to me, Xander, but I don't know if I can do that for you."

"I don't want you to do that for *me*. I want you to do that for *you*. You deserve to know the truth about life, about love. You deserve a happy future. With or without me. Will you do that?"

"You wish to inflict upon me that which I fear the most? Why should I promise you something which I dread? Why would you do that to me?"

"Because you're hurting, and I want to make you well."

She shook her head and made a derisory sound, but he pressed his finger to her lips.

"Wait, give me a chance to explain. Say, you have a fear of flying, how do you treat that?"

"Not by flying. That would only make it worse."

"You're right. But by showing you, little by little, that you have nothing to fear, and everything to gain. I'll show you how to change your thinking about it."

"And how will you do that?"

"By making you feel good." He pushed her hair from her face, and as his gaze roved over her face and he smiled so kindly at her, something melted inside. Fear. She wasn't afraid of him anymore. "There will be no pain, no uncertainty, no fear. Do you trust me?"

She nodded. There was nothing else she could do. In that moment she committed to him in a way she'd never done to anyone else before. She trusted him with that thing she revered the most—her innermost fears.

"Good." He stepped away from her. "We start tonight, after we reach the desert castle."

"Tonight?" Fear suddenly reached up and grabbed her again.

"Tonight, Ela. We will sleep close to each other, and, if you are willing, I will hold you in my arms. And that is all I will do. Tonight then?"

Despite his plans, she knew that he was asking permission to continue.

She nodded, and summoned up a brief smile. "Tonight," she confirmed.

But as she watched him walk away, she wondered what on earth she was letting herself in for. But, even as she wondered that, she felt calm inside. The calm was holding. At least for the time being.

CHAPTER 7

The desert sky at night usually comforted Elaheh, but not tonight.

Tonight, everything was too bright—from the star-sprinkled sky, to the lop-sided waning moon, no longer full but still shining too brightly onto the open plains which led to the desert castle of Havilah.

Elaheh bit her lip and stared out the car window, wishing the stony plains, burnished silver under the moonlight, would sink into the dark oblivion of the inky shadows which pooled beneath the rocky outcrops and be hidden from the world. And her along with it.

She didn't want anyone to see her.

She didn't want the world to bear witness to her fears.

She glanced at Xander who drove in silence, his narrowed gaze either looking directly ahead, or, occasionally, into his rear-vision mirror, to check his security team were still following. The lights from their cars confirmed their presence. Yet more lights in a world that seemed to be conspiring against her.

She looked out the window again. Despite the fact they were seated side by side, she felt distant from Xander, which was how she wanted to keep it. But she knew his intention was the opposite and it scared the hell out of her.

It had been easy to keep her fears at bay over the years—buried deep inside her, topped with the cement lid of her willpower—but that cement lid had been smashed by Xander. She'd gone over and over their conversation in her mind, trying to figure out how Xander had gotten her to tell him her secret. She'd decided she'd have been able to hold on to her secret if he hadn't touched her.

She closed her eyes at the memory of how that simple touch to her arm—a caress so gentle and yet so insistent— had sent an invisible charge which had broken her defenses and sent the truth pouring out, leaving her afraid and wanting to crawl into the darkness where no one could get to her.

She swallowed and folded her arms across her stomach, trying to settle the rapid beating of her heart and the queasiness in her stomach.

Then she felt his swift gaze upon her and she felt as exposed as if she lay naked on the star-lit plain. Their gaze tangled briefly before they both abruptly looked away.

"There's nothing to be afraid of, Ela," Xander said quietly, as they approached the looming outline of the castle. "I would never hurt you, or do anything you don't want to do. You know that, don't you?"

She nodded. He also had an uncanny way of knowing how she was feeling. Xander, the arrogant playboy, had hidden depths about which she knew nothing.

"Don't you?" He repeated the question, not seeing the movement of her head in the shadowy car.

"Yes," she said, because it was true. Despite all her profound fears she trusted Xander, or else she wouldn't have come. She cleared her throat. "Yes," she repeated, louder. "I do."

"Good," he said. She could hear his relief in the exhaled word. "We should arrive in five minutes."

Fear fluttered once more in her gut as she looked up at the castle, which grew larger with each passing mile. It was as dark as the sky was bright. But she knew it was a darkness which couldn't hide her, that she'd be more exposed than ever once she stepped inside.

The fortress origins of the desert castle were impossible to hide. It loomed over the desert plains like a threat, which was exactly what it was. It represented an ancient power of the Havilah kingdom when it had been one land —a power which Xander had in spades. A power he was using both to protect her and to challenge her. It seemed one went with the other and she couldn't stop it even if she wanted to. Because, bottom line, she knew he was right. She was still punishing herself for something bad that was done to her long ago. She knew it, but she didn't feel it. And it seemed Xander wanted to help her to feel it.

Xander drove through the gates which were opened by unseen people and promptly closed again. She'd never entered the castle through the gate before. Her visits had always been by helicopter which meant she'd never seen the power of the castle before.

The car doors banged shut with an echoing metallic clang around the apparently deserted courtyard. Dust hung in the air from the car's entrance, and dark shadows, cast by the soaring stone walls, loomed up on all sides. She paused for a moment and looked around. She was safe from external threat here—the writer of the threatening notes. She knew that. She was no longer in physical danger, but emotionally? She risked a quick glance at Xander who was waiting for her by the door, his eyes fixed on her, as if reading the very heart of her.

She took a long, slow breath of courage and walked towards him, focusing on his shoes. They were highly polished and the outside lights glanced off them. She stopped in front of him.

He lifted her chin with his finger and she looked up. He nodded. "That's better. I hate it when you look down."

"Why?"

"It's not you. It's not my fearsome Ela."

She opened her eyes wide, surprised at his possessive words. "You like me being fearsome?"

He brought his head closer to hers. A faint smile played on his lips. "I like *you*, being *you*."

She blinked as tears pricked her eyes. It was a strange compliment, not one she'd read about, but it got to her and it felt the most valuable thing anyone had ever said to her.

He stepped aside and indicated that she should enter the castle. She stepped into the great hall, brightly lit with flickering torches thrust into ancient wall sconces, and suddenly thought that the next time she stepped through these doors, she'd be a changed woman.

THE MORE TIME Xander spent with this different version of Ela, the more he believed he was doing the right thing.

As some of his staff approached Ela, she looked to him for reassurance. He winced inside. He hated seeing her this way.

"It's okay. You don't have to hide from anyone inside the castle. That's why we came here after all. It's totally safe. No one can enter or leave unless I say so, and all telecommunications are monitored."

She nodded, still appearing unsure, and he watched her follow the housekeeper and maid up the stairs to her room. As soon as she disappeared he turned to his butler.

"Whiskey, please. Make it a double." He pushed his fingers through his short hair. "Second thoughts, bring me the bottle."

"Certainly, Your Highness. Where do you wish me to bring it?"

"The first floor library."

For all its fortress-like origins, and more recent uses as a hunting lodge, certain rooms in the desert castle had been refurbished over a century earlier like a London club. Incongruous, maybe, but Xander had never felt so grateful as when he closed the door to the hall, and was surrounded by the familiar smell of leather, books, and polish. The narrow stone-framed windows looked out to the distant horizon, a thick navy line scoring the division between the starry sky and the darker hamada plains, whose contours were highlighted by the silver light. He briefly looked to the foothills of the mountain range before drawing the curtains across. He hated looking at that place where the old Bedouin camp had been, now deserted. It was a place which he never wanted to visit again, and which brought back memories which still managed to cut him to the core.

He looked up as his servant entered the library with the whiskey and a tray of snacks.

"Will Her Royal Highness, Queen Elaheh be joining you, sir?"

He hesitated. Ela wasn't the only one who was out of sorts. He shook his head. "No. We'll have dinner in an hour." An hour in which to gather his thoughts for the evening—and night—ahead.

ELAHEH TWISTED and turned in front of the mirror, frowning at the beautiful cerise satin evening gown which she'd selected from the wardrobe of clothes Shakira had thoughtfully sent over to the desert castle ahead of their visit.

It wasn't as demure and conservative as she usually wore, but bore all the hallmarks of Shakira's more extrovert taste. Elaheh rarely wore western clothes but Xander had made it clear that they'd be dressing for dinner so she knew that none of the other smart daywear would be suitable. At least Shakira had selected the more conservative clothes with their full length, high neckline and long sleeves. But it wasn't until she'd turned around and caught a glimpse of her rear view in the mirror that she realized the dress wasn't as demure as she'd first thought.

The satin caught the light, making the most of her petite curves in a way she didn't feel entirely comfortable with. But it was too late to change. She'd just have to make sure she didn't present her rear view to Xander. Then the light caught her breasts and she closed her eyes with embarrassment. This dress, she realized belatedly, was designed to seduce, regardless of how little bare skin was showing, or even, because of it. She didn't blame Shakira. Shakira breathed seduction—it was instinctive to her, and she wouldn't have been aware that the dress would make Elaheh feel so uncomfortable.

She stood biting her lip in indecision, and caught the eye of the maid looking back at her. She had to confide in someone.

"I'm not sure, maybe I should wear something else."

"I'm sorry, Your Majesty, but I've been informed that His Highness is expecting formal evening dress."

She knew why. He'd made it clear that tonight would be a special night when he'd begin his seduction of her. And she had agreed, hadn't she? She looked up into eyes that betrayed none of the courage with which Xander had attributed her. She blinked. This was ridiculous. She'd agreed to this, and she never reneged on an agreement. Nothing had changed. She still agreed that it was the way forward for her. So evening dress it was.

She tentatively fingered her newly curled hair which hung loose, like a cloak, providing her with some protection at least.. She shivered at the unfamiliar sensation of it against her skin. It made her feel a different person, which was what she wanted to be, wasn't it? She nodded to herself as if the person in the mirror had answered her question and, with a swish of the long bias-cut skirt, Elaheh resolutely turned her back on her image and strode over to the door.

Elaheh felt unaccountably nervous as she walked down the wide sweep of stairs to the great hall. The swish of the satin gown as it brushed against the polished stone sent further shivers of something like anticipation down her spine. If there were staff present, they were hidden, behind the wooden doors and stone walls, in remote areas of the castle, catering for the needs of the two crowned heads of state, but invisible. For that, Ela was grateful. She wanted as few people as possible to bear witness to her seduction.

The double doors of the dining room opened as if her approach was observed and yet she could see no one. Xander rose from the far end of a vast table set for only two people. She knew he rose because she saw him out of the corner of her eye. For some reason she seemed unable to look at him directly.

Torch lights flickered, reacting to the opening doors, but settling again as the doors closed behind her and the servants disappeared, leaving only Xander and her in the room.

"Ela," Xander greeted, his deep voice sending further shivers upon shivers across her skin.

She walked toward the first portrait and looked determinedly at it. "Xander," she replied, looking up at a portrait very different to that of his great grandmother. This man was austere and autocratic. "You look like him," she said, absorbing the strong lines of the man's face, and the piercing eyes.

He didn't reply but she heard him push a chair aside and his footsteps as he approached her. He stopped just short. She took a deep breath filled with his aftershave and something undefinably him. It did nothing to soothe her nerves.

"I should do. He was my great grandfather. It seems I've inherited the best of both my great-grandparents," he said with a grin. "The other portraits are of Amir and Zavian's families. A shared castle."

"Once a shared land," she murmured before turning to him.

"A shared land which paled in comparison to your own great and ancient lands of Tawazun."

She nodded, pleased by his acknowledgement of her country's superiority. It seemed he was trying to seduce her in more ways than the physical.

"My country is indeed great in size, but its growth has been stalled for generations."

He took a step closer to her, and she turned back to the portrait. "No longer, Ela. We will work together to make sure Tawazun moves into a new era of prosperity."

She smiled at the thought of the new world they were creating for her country and, taken off guard, turned to him. He was closer than she'd imagined. Her smile fell.

He reached out and brushed the side of her mouth. "You have a beautiful smile. You don't smile often enough."

She blinked in time to her suddenly rapidly beating heart. "I don't?" She didn't recognize her voice. It sounded breathless and husky at the same time, nothing like her usual forthright no-nonsense tone.

His finger lingered on her cheek, tracing the brackets created by a smile, which unaccountably had found its way back to her face. His smile broadened.

"No, you don't. But I'm hoping you will in the future."

"Why?" she asked again in that newly husky voice. "Who can say what will happen in the future?"

"Me. I can. The immediate future anyway."

And before she could react he tilted her chin gently up and kissed her. Life seemed to shift into a different, slower gear and she was acutely aware of ever nuance, every shift of his lips upon hers, his warm breath against her cheek. It lit up her body like a spark to a candle.

"Oh," she breathed, when he withdrew, his fingers still lingering against her cheek.

He sighed and stepped back. "Oh, indeed." He frowned, turning away, and she felt bereft, as if the sun had just slipped behind a black cloud, leaving her in cold shadow. Instinctively she placed her hand where his had been only seconds before.

He shot her a brief smile. He gestured toward the table. "Please, take a seat. Dinner has already been served. I wished us to be alone, without servants hovering."

She regained her senses and nodded, also brief. "Of course. We don't want word to get out."

He pulled out her chair, and she sat down, watching as he walked around the other side of the table, directly opposite. There would be no escaping his intense gaze.

He paused and then pulled in his chair, his hands steepling on the blackened oak table which was all the more beautiful for the marks of age it bore. "No word will get out, of that you can be assured. The staff have been hand-picked for this, and there is no possibility of them communicating without our knowledge. Every communication is being tracked. You are safe. No, the reason I wish us to be alone is an entirely personal one."

She raised an eyebrow but didn't dare speak in case it betrayed her nerves.

His eyes darkened as they met her gaze steadily. "Because I will be seducing you," he continued. "And I thought you'd prefer privacy."

She gave a brief nod of her head in agreement.

His lips quirked into a brief smile. "There's nothing to be nervous about, the only thing to anticipate is…" He hesitated as his thoughts coalesced into one word. "Pleasure."

She cleared her throat, reached out for her drink and took a sip. She placed it back on the table before replying. She, too, brought her steepled fingers together, her elbows resting on the table, her fingers tapping her lips. "You seem very sure."

"About giving you pleasure? Of course." He sat back in his seat, and looped one arm casually over the back of his chair.

"And you know this for a fact, do you? You assume all the women you've slept with have been in raptures of pleasure."

"Yes. Because, Ela, I'm not like other men. For me, there's no more pleasure to be gained than in giving pleasure to a woman. I listen, you see. I find out what women like, and I make sure I give it to them."

She really wished she'd hadn't pushed it because each word he uttered was said in a tone which caressed her nerves, because each word he uttered spoke a truth she knew to be true, because each word he uttered bypassed her defenses and stroked her, deep inside, sending flutters of anticipation to places she'd always refused to think about. It seemed being seduced by Xander required no thinking whatsoever.

She pressed her cool glass to her cheek, which flushed with anticipation. "So…" She sucked in a breath that did nothing to calm her thudding heart. "Do all women like the same thing?"

"No, you'd be surprised."

She was sure of it. "So, when does this seduction begin?"

"It's already begun." He took a sip of his wine. "Don't underestimate the seductive power of words."

She couldn't help wondering that if his words had this effect on her body, what state she'd be in when he touched her. Her blush deepened.

"But," he continued, "we must also eat." He gestured to the silver plates heaped with colorful appetizers of stuffed vegetables and spiced salads, and platters topped with elaborate silver cloches beneath which she could smell chicken and rice. "In the spirit of the caravanserai, I thought you might enjoy a traditional dinner. Please, help yourself. You must keep up your strength."

She look up at him through lowered lashes. It seemed her seductive instincts were kicking in, too. "And why's that?"

"Because, Ela, I don't intend to stop at words tonight. And, eating is also part of the seduction." He heaped some food on a spoon and offered it to her.

"Are you infantilizing me? Is that what seduction is?"

"Not at all. I can assure you that that is not the case. I am merely giving you something, and you are receiving it. Seduction 101."

"Seduction 101," she repeated. "And you think I'm learning from this?"

"No," he said to her surprise. "I am."

She should have resisted, she really should. But she found his reply as irresistible as his gaze and so she opened her mouth, the glossy red lipstick she'd previously applied now slightly smudged by the kiss.

His eyes narrowed. "Wider," he said and, with only a

moment's hesitation she opened her mouth wider. "Good." He slid the spoon onto her tongue and she closed her lips over it. It was her turn to witness how turned on he was. His lips opened as he gave a slight gasp. And, for the first time, she realized that she possessed a power of which she'd been completely unaware. She swallowed and slowly and deliberately licked her lips, watching him all the while. He sat back as if pushed.

"More," she said, not adding any words of courtesy. She needed him to know that she, too, could demand.

He scooped up another small mouthful and slid it onto her tongue. This time she closed her lips around the spoon as it slowly slid out. She noted with satisfaction that his hand shook a little.

With careful deliberation he dragged the empty spoon along her lips, and she let him. When he withdrew she licked her lips and he placed the empty spoon onto the plate with a clatter, and sat back.

She crossed her arms and rested them on the table, aware that the sheer satin clinging to her curves dipped to reveal the top of her breasts. She leaned towards him, her eyes narrowed. "I want more."

This time, he swept some food onto his finger, and extended it to her. She closed her mouth around his finger, her eyes so close to his that she could see they were dark with desire.

He shook his head with surprise as he watched her swallow.

"And what have you learned, Xander?

"Things I should have known already."

She leaned forward and licked his finger clean. "Like what?"

"That you are demanding, that you want control."

She raised an eyebrow. "And you will give it to me?"

"Of course not. You will have to work for it."

"And how do you propose I do that?"

"If you've finished eating, I suggest we adjourn to another, more suitable room."

She rose first. Food was the last thing on her mind now. "Suitable? For what?"

He held out his hand and she took it. He leaned and whispered in her ear. "For me to give you pleasure like you've never experienced before."

A bubble of desire burst inside her and she was shocked to find herself wet. She felt swollen and needy in the place which she'd vowed no man would ever know. But that was before she'd met Xander, before she'd put her trust so completely in him.

He squeezed her hand as if sensing her surprise. Then he pulled her to him, lifted her chin and pressed his lips to hers. He slid his tongue between her lips and swept her tongue. She gasped and opened her mouth wider to allow his tongue to explore her. She heard a groan and realized to her surprise that it was her own. Before she knew it her hands were around the back of his neck, making sure he couldn't retreat from the kiss, and she'd pressed her hips against his. The sensations further fanned the fire of need which nestled in the most secret parts of her body.

He pulled away too soon. He took hold of her hands and dragged them down between them. "Slowly, Ela."

She shook her head. "Indeed, not! I want more, now!"

"Ela. You are not to command. It is I who will command."

"You really expect me to surrender my will to you?"

"Yes, because you trust me, and because I will make sure the act of surrender will give you greater pleasure than it would do otherwise."

"I don't understand."

"No, but you will."

"Come." He tugged her hand and, for all his imperative of slowness, he walked quickly out the door, and she had to half-run to keep up with him. At the foot of the stairs he pulled her to him and she fell hard against him. He responded with a stormy kiss which had her panting with need.

"What now?" she asked.

"I want you to take off that fine dress and allow me to explore your body."

Her sex pulsed with a desire she didn't know she possessed. He wanted her naked in the hall? She didn't hesitate, but began to fumble with the straps of her gown.

He grinned and re-did the strap. "Not here, not now. Maybe some other time. But now I wish for privacy."

She gathered the skirts of her gown and they raced up the stairs. At his door, he pulled her to him and they kissed once more. Then he lifted her in his arms, pushed open the door with his foot and strode into his suite of rooms.

He set her down at the foot of the bed.

"And now, I wish you to take off your dress for me."

A flutter of something other than desire swamped her. He seemed to understand for he caressed her shoulders. "I will not touch you unless you want me to. I promise you that. You are safe. You must understand that. Unless you do, I will leave immediately because this is all about trust, and nothing about fear. Do you understand?"

And in that moment the fear left her. There was a silence in which things could have turned on a dime, could have gone either way. She knew that life would change for her forever, depending on her response. But, before she could think through the gravity of her decision, she'd nodded. "Yes." And spoken. It seemed her thought processes had been overtaken by something much stronger, much more demanding, much more ancient and persuasive than mere logic. "Yes," she repeated, louder, more sure.

He relaxed his grip and spun her around in his arms. "Good. In that case, it's time you undressed."

She must have betrayed her nerves because he squeezed her shoulders reassuringly. "It's up to you. All of it. You take control." He grinned. "I'm sure you don't mind doing that." The grin dropped. "Beginning by taking off your clothes."

CHAPTER 8

With trembling hands and a thumping heart Elaheh pushed the straps of her evening dress off her shoulders. She held his gaze, refusing to look away, despite the fact she knew her cheeks were as aflame as other parts of her.

She allowed the straps to slip lower, her dress barely held up by the swell of her breasts. She wondered if she should move, or whether he would. He didn't move. It was up to her, just as he said it would be. She had control. At least for now. She could do this.

His dark eyes raked her shoulders and the top of her breasts, before returning to catch her gaze, breathing hot life back into her frozen body.

Yes, she could do this, but more than that—despite the sick feeling that lurked in the pit of her stomach, despite the fears which gripped her head in a tight band—she *wanted* to do this. The need was alive in every fiber of her being, co-existing with her anxiety. Her mind battled with her body, warning her to stop but her desire charged her body with an electric current which over-rode the thoughts which struggled to protect her from harm.

Without breaking that gaze, she pushed the straps off her arms and the satin dress slithered past her breasts and fell in a ruffle around her hips, revealing her bra and stomach. She sucked in a deep breath as the warm air caught her bare skin.

As his eyes descended once more she gritted her teeth as she remembered the plain state of her underwear. Why did she never pay much attention to it? She had small breasts and her bra was white, plain and sheer, and not in the least seductive. Or so she thought. But then she saw him swallow and she realized that she didn't need a black lacy bra to seduce. The thought gave her confidence.

He flicked his gaze back up to hers. "May I touch you?"

She nodded. When the pad of his finger stroked her shoulder blade, slowly trailed across her collar bone to her throat and circled around the dip in her throat, she sucked in a sharp breath. His eyes immediately lifted to hers once more.

"Are you okay?" he asked, his voice huskier than she'd heard it before. It revealed a change in him which she hadn't anticipated. It was like something of his external self was breaking down, something she had caused. Her confidence increased another notch.

"Yes," she said. More than okay—much more—she could have added. But she was too intent on where his finger would move next to utter more than one word.

He continued to trace an invisible line down her chest before circling the soft swell of one breast and then another. She closed her eyes briefly as she tried to control her intense arousal which his touch ignited. The skin along which his finger moved had never been touched by a man and she felt impossibly naked, even though the dress still hung around her hips and her bra covered her breasts. She'd expected to be scared, instead she was thrilled.

"You, Ela," he said, nudging the material of the bra a little to reveal the edge of her nipple, "are so beautiful, it hurts my eyes." Desire tugged inside her.

"Close them, then," she said, with a husky purr she didn't recognize. It seemed that, despite her lack of experience, some things were instinctive.

His lips tweaked at the corners. "Okay, I'm in your hands."

Despite the flutter of nerves, Elaheh felt triumphant. There was no doubt about it, she liked being in control. Even if she had no idea what to do with it. He must have sensed her doubts.

"Do whatever you feel like, Ela. There's nothing you can do wrong, believe me."

She stepped toward him, pressed her nose to his chest and inhaled.

"What are you doing?"

"Smelling you. I like how you smell." That was the understatement of the year. He made her mouth water. Always had done, even if she'd refused to accept it. "You smell good."

He dropped a kiss on her head and also took a deep breath. "And so do you. You know, I always knew when you were near because of that lemony smell. What is it?" His sexily narrowed gaze locked onto hers.

She swallowed and shrugged. "Lotion, I guess. Locally made."

"Exotic, eclipsing all else around it—like you."

"Close your eyes again."

"Why?"

"I like it like that. I can behave more instinctively if you don't look at me."

He closed his eyes. "Your wish is my command."

"Hm." She'd smelled him, now she wanted to taste him. She raised herself onto tiptoes and licked his neck. She could see the effect as the muscles around his eyes contracted further, as he sought to control himself. "I like commanding a king."

"I think you like commanding everyone."

She smiled as she followed her impulse and trailed her tongue down from his neck onto his chest, burying her nose as low as she could get with his shirt buttoned, and inhaled deeply. She couldn't have described the innate maleness of the smell but it hit her at such a fundamental, animal level, she knew she needed more. She unbuttoned his shirt down to his navel, and forced herself to focus on what he'd said. "Of course, who doesn't like to command everyone."

"Not everyone, Ela, not everyone. You'd be surprised to learn that—"

His words were cut short as he took a sharp intake of breath, as she swept her hands across his chest and down, spanning her fingers so she could feel every dip and contour of his body. It felt forbidden, it felt like she was breaking down more than just the barriers between them, but something inside of herself.

Suddenly she plunged her fingers beneath the waistband of his trousers and felt the tip of his erection. She paused for a moment, then circled her finger around the head. It seemed to visibly swell beneath her touch. Power. She had it.

She stepped away and did what he had done, eyed him from top to toe. She liked what she saw. She smiled at his intense expression. "You were saying?"

"Nothing. I was saying nothing. You continue, do as you wish, because, for once, I believe it is me who will be commanded and I'll enjoy it all the more."

"Then you will indulge me?"

"Yes."

She turned around so she had her back to him, and flicked her hair over her breasts. "Undo my dress."

His fingers brushed her bare skin as he fumbled briefly with the zip, which was the only thing keeping her dress resting on her hips, before sweeping it down. She stepped out of the dress, her nerves returning as she turned around, dressed now only in her heels and underwear, which were neither luxurious nor the height of fashion. If he was amused at her plain bra and panties he didn't show it.

"You are so beautiful," he murmured.

She took a deep breath, trying to calm the pounding of her heart. She couldn't believe she was standing half-naked before him. But, even more, she couldn't believe how much it turned her on. She followed his gaze to her breasts where two needy nipples peaked with desire. It was just as well he couldn't see between her legs where her arousal was also fully evident.

"Now, it's your turn. I wish you to undress in front of me."

A short grin was followed by a bemused shake of the head and then he did as she commanded. With one swift movement he pulled his shirt over his head and tossed it aside. For a moment he stood with his hands on his hips surveying her from under a lowered brow, as if challenging her. She nodded, grateful for those few moments of stillness in which she could admire his chest and strong arms. The flat muscles in his body and his chest hair tracked downward in a tantalizing line. She looked down at his fly and then up at him.

"You may take off your trousers now, if you please."

"I do." With his answering gaze equally as steady, he unbuttoned his trousers and then pulled down his zip. His erection was released and pushed out from his shorts. She blinked lightly, trying to subdue a sudden flutter of fear. It was larger than she'd imagined. But before she could imagine any further he'd stepped out of both his trousers and shorts with one quick movement.

She couldn't prevent her hand from flying to her mouth. "Oh!" she gasped.

"I'm hoping that's a good 'oh', and not a disappointed one," he said, with a confident smile which showed that he wasn't accustomed to disappointing.

She shook her head. "No, not disappointed. More surprised. It's quite… large."

His smile faded as if suddenly understanding her concern. "Don't worry. It's not going anywhere you don't want it to go. Remember that. You have the power and control here. For now, at least," he added, with a glimmer of a smile in his eyes.

She nodded, but for the life of her she couldn't figure out what she wanted to do next. Her vision seemed to be filled with only one, very erect, thing. It caught at her intention, and pressed unwelcome memories against her consciousness, nudging them, willing her to turn away and run.

He frowned, as if picking up on some of her anxiety. "I'll put my shorts on again. Yes?"

She nodded. "Yes, please. It's just…" She trailed off.

"You don't have to explain anything." He was as good as his word and was soon covered. "Now, do you want to proceed?"

"Yes, it's just"—she shrugged—"I don't know what to do."

"Okay, would you like me to take the lead?"

"Yes please."

"Good."

She loved the way his lips formed the word good. She tried to kiss him, but he shook his head.

"Not yet. In a little while maybe. After I've given you some pleasure."

She liked the sound of that.

"Now, remember, you can stop at any time."

"Stop what?"

"Stop me from doing what I'm about to do to you." He pressed his finger to her open lips. "And before you can ask what I'm about to do to you, remember, trust me."

She bit her lip but nodded. She felt at war with herself but her body's needs were winning once more.

He lifted skeins of her thick hair and rubbed it between his fingers. "You have beautiful hair. You should always wear it down when we are together, like this."

She nodded, again. At that moment she felt as if she were in some kind of thrall to him and would do anything. So much for being in control. It seemed that surrendering a little of that control—or a lot—gave her a surprising amount of pleasure.

Then all thought vanished into a puff of air as he lowered his lips, not to her waiting ones, but to her neck. His lips and breath were warm against her skin and tickled it as he trailed kisses under her ear. He groaned and lifted his head. "You smell delicious."

She would have returned the compliment if she'd been capable of forming words. But all she could do was to lift her chin and offer her neck again. It seemed she'd conveyed her message sufficiently as his lips descended once more. This time she felt the smooth trailing of his tongue as, instead of moving to her other ear, he moved down to her breasts which rose with a sharp intake of breath to meet his lips. She closed her eyes as she absorbed the sensation of his lips and tongue against her delicate skin. The feelings were unexpected and all encompassing. She cradled his head and kissed the top of his dark hair as his clever tongue continued to work its magic.

She felt his finger move along the edge of her bra and slip under its edge. He looked up. "May I?" he asked, as if he were about to top up her drink. She nodded. "Yes," she breathed.

He needed no further encouragement and slipped his finger under her bra, his fingertip catching her erect nipple, causing her to gasp. His eyes were fixed on her to assess her reaction. Even he couldn't have anticipated that she would react in quite such an extreme fashion.

The gasp turned noisier as he fingered her nipple under her bra. At the same time the exquisite sensations were centered on her breasts, deep inside of her, the same sensations were stirred—moistening her and sending ripples of pleasure as if he were somehow stroking her inside. She surrendered herself to the pleasure for only a few moments because the more she gained, the more she wanted.

She fumbled behind her to unhook her bra. She wanted nothing between his fingers and her skin. She grunted with frustration.

"Allow me," Xander said with a grin. With one deft movement which was far more practised than Elaheh wanted to consider, she was free of the bra. But, instead of paying immediate attention to her freed breasts, he stepped away. For an awful moment she thought he wasn't going to continue, as if ridding her of her bra was all he was going to do. But then, with one swift movement, she found herself in his arms, being carried to the bed. He sat down with her nestled in his lap and kissed her in a way which showed that her that he had no intention of stopping.

She moaned as their tongues met in a dance whose beat quickened with each pulse of her heart. She wanted to be closer and shifted on his lap, but still she wanted her flesh pressed against his. She broke off the kiss and opened her legs, kneeling either side of his hips so she could rub her bare breasts against his chest as she pressed her lips back to his again.

She was panting now, as they kissed, her nipples stimulated against his chest hair. And, as she moved against his chest, her hips also moved in a circular motion, caressing the erection which, while covered, was still very much in evidence. All fears were forgotten.

She pulled away from the kiss with a gasp and arched

her neck away, as she focused on the intense sensations which were growing as she rubbed against him, adjusting her stance as she figured out which part of her was giving her pleasure.

He kissed and tasted her neck as she closed her eyes, surrendering herself to the sensations which washed through her in waves, quickening. Then he lifted her breasts into his hands and rubbed her nipples. A gasp tore from her lungs as the sensations amplified inside. She didn't know what was happening to her, she had no idea what to do apart from what her body was dictating to her. She felt she was being urged on, but had no idea as to the destination.

It was only when she felt the warm, wet heat of his mouth around her breast and nipple that the tensions intensified and she knew she needed release from the thrall which held her. She rubbed herself against him harder and thrust her breast into his mouth. She could feel the wet in her panties soaking against his shorts but didn't care. She needed more, she needed to continue to get whatever lay at the end of this sensation.

He moved from one breast to the other. Still she panted and moved against him, caught in a fever pitch of desire but with no knowledge where to go next.

Then he licked his finger and touched her and she stopped mid movement. He touched her there, that place which felt like the nub of her desire. He slid his finger beneath her soaking panties and rubbed her and caressed her. It was all she needed to shift to that place she needed to go.

She cried out as white-hot shimmers and pulses and flutters filled her. Then she called out his name as the shimmering movement inside her slowed and drained her. She slumped against him, suddenly exhausted, but sweetly so.

"Oh, Xander," she breathed. "I had no idea."

He cupped her face and kissed her. "No idea?"

"That such pleasure existed. I thought…" She trailed off and swallowed as the reality of what she'd thought for so long hit her. Tears pricked her eyes. "I thought sex was about pain, not pleasure."

His lips twisted and he shook his head as if trying to deny what she'd just said. "No," he said.

She nodded her head "Yes." And then she leaned against him, cradled in his arms and the tears, so long held back, flowed against his chest, while he cradled her head and kissed her hair and murmured soothing words.

It had taken a long while for Ela to cry herself out. And Xander hadn't moved until she'd finished. He didn't want to break the spell, because it felt like a healing spell and he instinctively knew that it was what she needed.

But now, as Xander lay listening to the old grandfather clock in the library strike one, with Ela nestled in his arms asleep, like a delicate, damaged bird, he knew three things.

One, there was little he could do about his erection without waking her and that he wouldn't do.

Two, something had healed for Ela tonight.

Three, watching Ela heal had shattered the seal he'd set over his emotions. It had awoken something deep inside of him which scared him to death.

~

Xander awoke the next morning to an empty bed and a bad mood. He could deal with his physical arousal in a time-honored way, but he knew it wouldn't satisfy him.

Ela. Something might have healed for Ela last night, but it had opened a can of worms for him.

He swung his legs off the bed, pushed his fingers through hair which didn't need to be pushed off his face and rose with purposeful steps, pulled on his shorts, and made for the gym. If he couldn't have a woman then he'd have to sweat it out another way.

But even after a workout, a cold shower and a meeting with his advisors his mood was still black. He found himself on a video call to the only other person in the world who would understand.

"Xander," said Roshan, leaning in to adjust his settings before sitting down, his forearms on his thighs as he sat alert and looking directly at Xander, as if to assess his mood. "What's up?"

"Ela is what's up."

Roshan sighed, shook his head and sat back in his chair. "What's happened now?"

Xander opened his mouth to speak but couldn't continue. What was he going to say? He felt sorry for her? She was more than he'd imagined? "She's just... demanding too much of me."

"Of course she is. That's just her. Just ignore it."

"It's hard when it's..." He trailed off. How could he describe what had happened last night?

"It's what?"

"When it's kind of personal... I guess," he added lamely.

Roshan leaned forward, and Xander didn't like the

spark of interest which lit his eye. "Personal, eh? Don't tell me you've succumbed to Elaheh's charms."

Xander grunted but couldn't deny Roshan's statement. He never lied to his brother—from the early days after they'd lost their parents they'd made a pact to always be honest with each other. "She's beautiful, I'll give you that, and every now and then I catch a glimpse of the woman who exists behind that stroppy mask. But the bottom line is she's driving me mad." Xander hoped that by diverting Roshan from his statement he'd avoid it. But the look on Roshan's face indicated the opposite.

Roshan nodded. "I see."

Xander scowled.

Roshan pressed his lips together and shook his head. "It was fifteen years ago, Xander. You've got to move on."

Xander felt his anger crumble away and tears prick his eyes as Roshan dove straight to the heart of the issue. He licked his lips and tried to speak but no words came out. He blinked instead.

"Selya was my friend, Roshan. More than my friend. We were always meant for each other. She was the only girl I ever loved, the only girl for me. I still..." He petered out, unable to express how he still lived daily with the feeling that there was a hole in the place where his heart should have been. His heart, that had been gouged out of his body, and tossed aside for the desert sun and crows to eat the day that his love had been killed before his eyes, alongside his parents. Even now he unconsciously rubbed his hand where her blood had splattered.

"I know, Xander, but you can't live in the past."

"It's not the past to me."

"It has to be. Unless you leave it behind, you will have no future. Xander, listen to me, you can do it."

"It's hard, Roshan. *So* hard."

"I know. You were always the soft one, always the tender, the sensitive, the vulnerable. And it seems your love for Selya was planted deep at an early age. I understand that. But you still have a loving heart."

Xander made a scoffing sound.

"Don't dismiss that, Xander. I know you do. If you didn't you wouldn't have made this call to me. I understand, probably more than you know. And"—he glanced to where Xander guessed Shakira was standing—"now I share my life with my love I *truly* understand. It will happen again for you. Don't let the past become a barrier to your happiness." He gave someone a heart-stopping grin and Xander felt a shift in his own heart. Then Roshan turned back to him. "And, you know, I think Elaheh might be just the person to force you to find your heart."

"I'm not letting Elaheh loose with my heart. Who knows where it will end up."

"Maybe, maybe not, but she sure has the force to batter down your defenses, and that's what's needed right now. And, I suspect, it's a process which she's begun already. Anyhow, I have to go. Take care, and call me soon."

Xander logged off and sat back in his chair, looked up at the ceiling and blinked. It was good to talk to Roshan. It eased the pain of his loss a little. But as to the rest? It was nonsense, except for Elaheh being forceful enough to kick down his defenses. He'd have to watch that.

CHAPTER 9

"No," Xander said, the next morning. "It's out of the question."

"But," pouted Elaheh, replacing her tea cup and reaching out for his hand across the breakfast table. "You asked me what I wanted to do, and going into the desert is what I want to do." He took her hand in his but his frown didn't disappear as she'd hoped. She tossed her napkin onto the table and rose, watching as his eyes were drawn to her as if to a magnet. She could get used to this. She walked around the table and leaned over his shoulder, pressing her breasts to his back, and kissed his cheek. "Didn't you mean it when you said we could do anything I wished?"

He huffed a frustrated sigh. "Of course I did." He twisted around and caught her lips in a brief but devastating kiss. It was nearly enough to make her forget what she wanted. Nearly, but not quite. "I thought you'd want something reasonable, to do something inside the castle, where it's safe."

"My request *is* reasonable. You love the sea and we spent a morning at the beach. And I love the desert, and would like to spend some time there. That's reasonable and fair."

"We *are* in the desert."

"We're in a castle—" interrupted Elaheh.

"A *medieval* castle—" corrected Xander.

"A medieval castle with all the trappings of a luxurious palace."

Xander shrugged. "What do you have against luxury? I, for one, enjoy it."

She desperately wanted him to want what she wanted. But, it seemed, they were opposites. He loved the water and the sea, she hated it. She loved the dry desert heat, and it appeared he hated that. At night they'd found mutual pleasure but, it seemed, their differences were all too obvious in the cold light of day.

"I'm a simple Bedouin woman who feels most at home in the desert. That's all."

Xander grunted. "There is nothing simple about you, Queen Elaheh."

She pouted again. She liked the way his gaze slid to her lips as if he wanted to kiss them. "You call me by my full name and title when you're cross with me."

"I'm not cross with you. It's only..."

"It's only nothing. You obviously have no real objection, so why don't we stop arguing and get going?" She grinned. "I've given instructions to ready the horses and prepare the camp ahead of us. And don't worry, while we'll *feel* alone, I've taken the liberty of ensuring we'll be safe. Your men won't be far away."

"You've what?" Xander exploded. "Ela!"

She pressed her finger against his lips. "It's okay. We'll be safe." She moved her finger over his lips and she knew she had him when he licked her finger. It didn't take a mind-reader to figure out where his thoughts were straying. She took a calming breath. As much as she was tempted, she wasn't about to be diverted from her plans. Besides, there would be plenty of time to experience all Xander had to offer in the desert. "The desert will be just that—deserted, or mostly. We can do whatever we choose to do." She raised a suggestive eyebrow.

His eyes darkened in a dangerous and seductive warning. "And where, exactly, is our destination?"

"The Shuruq Alshams Wahah."

"Sunrise Oasis," said Xander, giving it its western name. "And no further?"

"Maybe. Maybe not." The Sunrise Oasis wasn't her ultimate destination, but she decided not to tell him where they'd spend the night. It was further away and would no doubt elicit an even more negative response. They'd have no choice but to continue on if they wanted a tent to sleep in.

"Okay, but no further."

"Great! You'll enjoy it, you'll see," she added. And she really did hope he would see, because she yearned for the intimacy of the night before. The pleasure he'd given her was turning out to be a drug—once tasted the cravings only increased, demanding satisfaction. Well, she had the prospect of a full day and night alone with him and she knew Xander wouldn't be able to refuse those particular demands.

· · ·

XANDER COULD HAVE STOPPED the expedition to the desert oasis. Of course he could. But it seemed he was unable to deny Ela anything. Watching her natural passions emerge the previous night had had an effect on him he didn't wish to consider. As they walked through the castle to prepare themselves for the horse ride ahead—he tried not to shudder at the idea of the ride—her animated face was reward enough for his sacrifice. At least they were venturing no further than the Shuruq Alshams Oasis.

Ela might believe he had no valid reason not to enter the desert, but he did have one. Only one. But one big enough with the potential to derail him completely if he returned to the place where his nightmare had begun.

ELAHEH FELT the thrill of the ride in every cell of her newly awakened body. The desert wind had pushed her hijab from her face and her hair flew out behind her. And for once she didn't care how it looked. The early morning sun was warm on her face, and her stallion was at his responsive best. They galloped as one, the pounding of his hooves in time with her quickened heartbeat. She was relaxed, and yet fully aware, living in the moment in a way she couldn't do when she was in the public eye. And she was always in the public eye.

She glanced across at Xander who, despite his protestations, looked superbly at ease on his mount. He might not be enjoying it, but he was certainly good at it. The thought suddenly crossed her mind that she didn't know anything he wasn't good at. If she had been asked to name one weakness in him, she wouldn't have been able to. But surely no one was that strong? There were times she sensed an unease in him, but she had no idea as to its source. But maybe, just maybe, by putting him out of his comfort zone she'd be able to know him a little better. Especially if she bypassed the Shuruq Alshams Oasis and headed directly to the place she really wanted to go. She suspected he wouldn't be aware of the change in itinerary.

And she was correct. While the desert was apparently featureless, she knew her way instinctively, drawn to the smudge on the horizon which indicated her destination. And Xander said nothing, merely rode silently alongside her.

Slowly the smudge took shape. Firstly the spiky leaves of the palm trees—their points dark against the deep blue sky on the horizon. Then the different shades of brown and green, then the birds who lived there. It was only as they approached that the mirage of shimmering water turned into the actual water of the oasis.

The land was a kind of no man's land now and so only the most traditional Bedouin would use it. But not at this time of year. She knew it would be empty, and had taken precautions to make sure it was before they'd set off. The place had been secured and prepared for their arrival. Although she'd protested against the luxury of the castle, she was anxious to make sure Xander was comfortable. Both for himself, and for her. The more at ease he was, the more satisfaction he could give her, she thought with a smile.

As soon as they reached the first trees she jumped down and patted her horse, calming him after the brisk gallop.

Xander jumped off his horse and looked around.

"Strange, I remember the Shuruq Alshams oasis as being smaller."

Elaheh smiled, suddenly uneasy. She shouldn't have tricked him, but this oasis was so beautiful that surely he'd forgive her once he understood where they really were.

He was frowning as he looked around. He started to walk toward the Roman ruins, hidden by the lush trees, which would betray the identity of the oasis. Elaheh's heart beat quickly in panic as she realized that her stay would be cut short unless she did something quickly. She shot out her hand and grabbed his. It seemed she'd have to begin where she'd intended to end.

"Let me show you where we'll be staying."

For a moment she didn't know if he'd agree, but then he glanced at her and his expression softened—changed from suspicion to warmth.

"It seems I can't deny you anything," he said with a smile.

"And that's,"—she grinned back—"as it should be."

Elaheh led him through the towering palms which hid the waters of the oasis and climbed up a narrow path to a tent which had been erected in the prime location, overlooking the verdant oasis, complete with Roman ruins of the ancient spa, now hidden by the tent.

She ran ahead and opened the rear curtain of the tent. She gave an exaggerated bow. "My sheikh," she said with bowed head.

Xander walked through to the tent and she followed, watching as he absorbed all the fittings she'd instructed—principally the bed. Everything else was minimal, but the bed was fitted with luxuriant silk in all the rich colors Elaheh secretly loved—aubergine, copper, purples, reds—

it looked like a jewel set in the bleached tones of the desert. She followed him inside and let the curtain fall. She was relieved to see the front entrance was still covered. Their location remained a secret. She'd deal with that later. After she'd got what she wanted.

He turned to her. "Looks like a scene for a seduction," he said, a slight frown playing on his brow. For a moment she doubted her abilities to seduce. "But who's seducing who?" he murmured. He approached her and thrust his fingers through her hair, his thumb stroking her cheek. Her doubts immediately evaporated. "Looks like my pupil has overcome her fears."

She nodded, liking the way his fingers moved against her scalp. "I have, thanks to you." She kissed the palm of his hand. "You showed me what true pleasure was like." She held his dark gaze. "And I want more."

He smiled, that rare smile. "Then, Ela, I will give you more."

"Good, because I want… a lot more."

He raised an eyebrow. "Anything in particular?"

She licked her lips, suddenly nervous at what she was about to ask.

"Go on," he said gently. "Anything you want is okay by me."

"I want sex. Full sex." She paused but he didn't reply. "I want you inside me," she said for clarification in case he hadn't understood. But the darkening in his eyes didn't lighten.

"No."

"No?" She wasn't sure she'd heard right.

"That's right, the answer is no. You need to save that for your husband."

She ground her teeth in frustration. "I didn't realize you were so old-fashioned."

"I am when it comes to you." He sighed, and caressed her shoulder. "Look, I want to help you. You suffered an experience no woman—certainly no girl—should endure."

His words stung. "You only doing what you're doing to help me? Not because you want to?"

He gave a low laugh. "I didn't have you down for insecure."

"I'm not, but even so..." She looked away and was pleased when he caught her chin and tilted her to face him once more.

"Even so, you're a woman who wishes to be desired. And, believe me, you are. I did want to help you. I wanted to show you that not all men are alike, not all men want to hurt, some want to give, some want to pleasure. But somewhere in the middle of doing that, my feelings have changed." He paused as if he were struggling to find the right words. She decided to take pity on him.

"And if I were a woman who no longer needed help?"

He smiled. "I'd still desire you." The smile dropped. "I'd still want to pleasure you, to see your eyes close as you surrender to your passion."

"Um, I like the sound of that." She lifted herself onto tiptoe and kissed him. By the time she lowered herself once more, his gaze had heated up, and she decided it was worth another try. This time she decided a more physical approach might work.

She smoothed her hand down his chest and lower, until it brushed the front of his trousers. His eyes narrowed. "Ela," he said in a warning tone.

She opened her eyes wide. "What?"

"We are not having full sex, no matter what you might think."

She crossed her arms. "Really! All I want is sex with you. I didn't realize it would be quite so hard to get. I understood that men were happy to poke it"—she glared down at his obvious erection—"anywhere."

"I don't know who you've been talking to, but I can assure you I'm choosy where I—to use your charming expression—poke it."

She felt hurt, and blinked as the strange sensation filled her. "I'm really not attractive enough for you, am I?" Her voice sounded strangely weak and hoarse. She tried to clear her throat but there was a big lump which wouldn't budge. She tried to pull up the scarf which had slipped from her hair on the ride, but he stopped her, and dragged it away further from her hair and face. He cupped her cheeks with both his hands and looked into her eyes.

"You're wrong, Ela. I find you very attractive."

She gulped. "Even when I'm haranguing you?"

He gave a light shrug. "You infuriate me then, but I still can't help my body responding, as it is now. No, I find you very attractive. Come closer and I'll show you just how much."

She couldn't have denied him, or herself, if she'd wanted to, and she most certainly didn't want to. So she stepped forward into his arms and he caressed her back and then lower, before carefully taking off her abaya. Then he carried her over to the bed and laid her down. He lifted the light dress she wore beneath her abaya and stroked up her leg, caressing her thigh. She shivered and closed her eyes. The effect of his caress was surprising, more than surprising. It was as if he'd flicked a switch which had ignited other switches, sweeping over and inside her body, turning them on, one at a time. She still didn't open her eyes because she was afraid to see what this turning on had done to her body. Every part of her felt hyper aware, as if tuned in to a higher frequency.

Then his other hand swept up her other leg. His thumbs curved around her thighs and touched the most intimate part of her. This time she did open her eyes and she was met with the darkened, aroused eyes of Xander. The more he touched her, the more she wanted him completely—inside her. Wantonly, she opened her legs wide and lifted her dress. He needed no further invitation and pulled down her panties. When he touched her she gasped, as he toyed with her moist skin.

"You see," she gasped again, "I'm ready for you to be inside me."

"You might be ready, but I'm not entering you."

"Please," she asked, unable to deny the throbbing deep inside of her.

"Um, I like the way you say 'please'. Maybe…"

"Yes?" she asked hopefully.

"Maybe there is a way."

"How?"

"I'll give you what you desire only if you surrender your will to me. Only then will I oblige."

He'd gone too far! "I won't surrender my will to anyone!"

He withdrew his thumbs which has been caressing her in a most exciting kind of way. She clamped her hands on his to stop him from moving.

"Then you won't get what you want," he replied, his

lips twisted into a sexy smile, as if he knew she'd refuse, as if he'd wanted her to refuse. "And you'll have to be content with a little appetizer."

"What are you going to do?"

"You'll see."

"But—"

"Ela, be quiet."

She didn't say another word because there wasn't anything else she wanted to say as his hands resumed their exploration of her. He no longer lingered around her sex but, instead, his hands swept over her hips, and onto her flat stomach. Then he lowered his head and kissed her bellybutton. She squirmed with pleasure.

"Why did that feel so good?" she asked, suddenly aware that her breathing had quickened.

"Be quiet, Ela," he commanded in an easygoing kind of way, his breath hot against her bare skin. And, apart from the gasp, as his tongue tracked downward, she was.

She wondered what he was going to do and the anticipation had her on edge. She gasped as his tongue found the source of her need and lapped her as if she were the most exquisite drink and he was dying of thirst in the desert.

She gripped the bed clothes in both fists and arched back, her hips coming into closer contact with his face. In response to her intense reaction he suckled her and instantly she was flooded inside with an intense combination of heat and warmth and intense pleasure, the like of which she'd never experienced.

"Oh, Xander!" she gasped. "That's wonderful."

He lifted his head to look at her. "Ela," he growled. "Will you stop talking!"

She clamped her mouth shut, not wanting to argue in case he stopped doing these things to her. He resumed his ministrations and she soon forgot about talking as the coiling sensations intensified again and all her thoughts and feelings were centered on the rush of pleasure which soared through her body. And then his finger circled where she wanted him, teasing her, and she opened her legs more fully. He slid his finger inside of her and she cried out as she became swamped by powerful sensations which surged through her repeatedly in waves, making her gasp and focus on the pleasure which his tongue and fingers brought.

Her fingers tingled and inside… well, inside it blew away not just her breath but her mind, and in that instant she knew a freedom she'd never known before. And she knew that she'd always be working towards possessing that freedom again.

As the echoes of her orgasm rolled away, she lay back on the bed blinking, as if she'd emerged into a whole new world. And her first view of this whole new world was filled by Xander's face.

"You should have sex with me now," she said, unable to stop herself.

His expression of male satisfaction faded. "It's usually called making love. At least it is when two people are in this situation." He swept his hands along her legs and sat back.

"You should make love to me now." She was prepared, after all, to compromise up to a point. She dropped her eyes to his trousers. "It's clear you want to."

"It is," he said standing up. "And it should also be clear to you by now that I don't intend to."

She couldn't remember the last time she hadn't been obeyed. She rose and walked over to him, and slid her hands onto his straining erection. He closed his eyes and sucked in a breath between closed lips. Then he opened his eyes and glared at her. "Ela! You are not getting your way over this." He removed her hands. "Unless, that is, you wish to surrender your will to me, here and now, and do everything exactly as I say? Hm?"

For a moment she had the impulse to go to him and be that subdued woman he wanted, to place her hands on his shoulders and shift them down his arms and lay her cheek against his broad chest. There was relief in that thought of surrender to someone who was strong to take her cares away. Then the image of her mother flashed into her mind—someone biddable who'd been outbid by other women. If you were weak, you lost, she reminded herself. She shook her head.

He smiled again. He'd won and he knew it. It was clear, now, that he didn't want her to surrender her will to him. "Then I suggest we eat the feast which I can smell has been provided for us."

"And then to bed?"

"Yes, of course."

As she walked around the tent picking up her clothes from where they'd fallen and putting them back on again, she realized she felt different. She was more aware of her body, she thought abstractly. Before it had been something which housed her will and her brain. Now… she couldn't quite describe it, which annoyed her. She liked to be able to analyze things and people. It wasn't until later, when she lay in bed after being thoroughly pleasured that she realized her body had awakened a will which was every bit as demanding as her mind. The battle had begun —not only between her and Xander—but between her mind and her body.

IN THE END Xander had decided eating was over-rated. It seemed Ela was determined to divert him. There was no way he was going back on his word, but when she wanted to pleasure him, as he'd pleasured her, he decided a little compromise was in order.

Sometimes, he considered—as Ela stroked and caressed him with her fingertips, her whole hand, and then, surprisingly, her mouth—a proactive, dominant woman could be exactly what a man required.

It was only later, after Ela had satisfied and pleasured him as thoroughly as he had her, and she lay curled in his arms, fast asleep, as if drugged from giving and receiving pleasure, that he realized something had changed inside of him.

He felt different. He closed his eyes as he considered what it was that had changed. He could smell her sweet fragrance, could feel her delicate skin and bones under his fingertips, and could feel the beating of both her heart and his, as if they were merged, as if they were one thing.

He froze. *One thing.* She'd broken him down, that was what she'd done. But he didn't want to feel anything, did he? Because that way opened him up to the opposite of pleasure—exposed him to pain. Something he knew only too well.

Gently he disengaged from Ela's body, sat on the edge of the bed—its colorful silks and satins now disheveled and half-discarded on the woven rugs which lined the floor of the tent. He put his head in his hands and closed his eyes. What had he done? His heart thudded as he pressed his hands against his temples. The blood pumped around his body, mocking his belief that he'd managed to extinguish life at the very heart of him. He'd thought his emotions were so repressed, he'd made them extinct. It seemed he was wrong.

He stood up and strode to the front of the tent and gripped the curtains which barely moved in the stillness of the morning. He needed to break this feeling, shut it down before it destroyed him. He needed air and light.

With one swift movement he push aside the curtains and stepped out, expecting to see nothing but the emptiness of the desert to soothe his soul. Instead, he was confronted with the ruins of the Roman spa and the beauty of the oasis which was engraved on his mind. It had once been a favorite escape for the royal family and their closest friends. And so it had been on that night when his parents and beloved friend were killed before him and Roshan. The night his life had ended. The night his new life, without emotion, had begun.

Suddenly he felt a hand on his shoulder.

"What is it?" Ela asked. "What's wrong."

He didn't turn to her but continued to look, unseeing, at the beauty and the pain that lay before him. It was as if the shroud which had enveloped his fear and sadness had suddenly dissolved, leaving nothing but the pulsating beat of a bleeding heart—a bleeding heart through which he felt two things.

One the sadness had not lessened over time, but, if anything, had become more painful. And two, his need for this woman—this infuriating, opinionated, arrogant woman—had become more acute. And both were now inextricably linked together. It seemed he couldn't have the one without acknowledging the other. And he knew the reason why. Because they both probed and prodded that poor thing he'd used to call his heart.

He had a choice. He could ignore both, or embrace both. And, at that moment he had no idea what to do.

Then he felt her hand touch his. He closed his eyes in response, as if trying not to allow anyone to see into his eyes where the feelings might be seen. He bit his lip and kept his eyes closed and didn't respond to her hand. But it curled around his anyway. If she'd done anything else— spoken again, put her arms around him, demanded a hungry kiss—he thought he could have refused. He'd have been able to meet her energy with a heavy dose of his own. But she didn't.

"Xander." She spoke his name in a whisper, like the wind through the trees. He squeezed his eyes shut more tightly, as he felt the pull of her voice through his body. He couldn't let her affect him. He couldn't. That way led madness. "Xander." The word came again, slightly stronger, but with doubt this time. It was the doubt that did it. He fluttered open his eyes and turned to look at her.

She looked different—stripped bare, literally, but not just her body, whose petite curves were heightened by the shadows shimmering through the palm trees. But in her eyes, too. As if their lovemaking had stripped her of her coverings, leaving the real Ela naked and bare before him. He frowned, and brushed her hair from her face.

"You are so beautiful."

She gave a small smile. She looked so young. He smiled

back and kissed her gently on the lips. Not in the hot, sensuous way they had been kissing but with tenderness. He suddenly realized that everything had changed with that one act. He frowned.

She frowned back. "Is something the matter?"

He had to talk. He had to be honest with her, he knew that much. "It would have been all right if we hadn't come here." He gestured outside the door to the beautiful oasis full of memories.

"I'm sorry, I was selfish, I wanted to come so much. It's so beautiful. I... didn't think you'd mind once you'd seen it."

He grimaced, but his hand didn't leave her face, his fingers pushed through her hair, holding her steady as his thumb swept her cheek. "It's not that." He glanced outside, seeing its beauty but not appreciating it. How could he, when all he could see was the dark spreading stains of the blood shed by his parents and beloved on the white sand?

"What is it, Xander?" she asked "What's wrong...?"

He shook his head, trying to rid himself of images ingrained in his mind and heart, images he'd thought he'd forgotten. "It holds memories—bad ones."

"Tell me."

He swallowed as he tried to form the pain into words which wouldn't hurt.

"It was here that my parents died. It was here that they were killed. And, alongside them, the girl I'd loved since I was a child, the girl I was to marry." He turned to her. "They died instantly. They did not suffer."

She reached out to touch him, to reassure him with instinctive sympathy.

"Unlike you and Roshan," said Ela gently.

"Roshan was tougher than me. He took it on the chin. He internalized it and it made him stronger. But me"—he gave a rueful smile—"I'm not made of such stern stuff and ran away as soon as I could. I couldn't wait to leave Sharq Havilah, but it seems, my love for my country cannot be avoided. I thought I'd managed to escape its clutches for a while, but it was stronger than I imagined."

"You were younger, he spent less time with your family. You were more lost than Roshan."

Xander shrugged. "Whatever, that's the past. I'd rather talk about the present."

"It's not the past," said Ela, shaking her head. "It's still very much part of your present, and by the looks of things, influencing your future."

Xander flicked his hand and looked away uncomfortably. "Don't try to psychoanalyze me. For one thing I don't need it, and for another you know nothing about my past."

"I know enough to understand that you are still hurting."

"Of course I am. And I always will. The only girl I loved, or ever will love, died that day, and so did my heart." He took a deep breath. "I think it's time to leave, Elaheh."

Silence filled the tent. For once, it seemed, Ela had nothing to say. Which was good. Because neither had he. What he'd said he'd always believed. And he still did, didn't he? But as the seconds passed, as Ela withdrew her hand from him, leaving the loneliness of his pain even emptier, the doubt crept in, swiftly quashed by the cool rigor of his will, just as he'd been doing ever since that fatal night. No, it was best like this. He remained where he was, even as he heard Ela move around the tent behind him, getting dressed, hiding the passion of their night together.

Not once during the ten minutes in which it took Elaheh to dress and gather her things, did Xander turn to her, or look her in the eye. He'd said his piece and she knew he'd meant it. He'd closed down their relationship before it had begun because of the past. But it was too late for her. Xander had changed her and there was no going back now. She wanted him, whether he loved her or not.

And, now, he was looking out, once more, over the oasis before them to the distant horizon. She understood it was easier than facing his pain. Her eyes were drawn to the planes of his face, shaded by the low sun which filtered through the trees. A few weeks ago she would look upon that arrogant, handsome face, and become incensed. There were traces of that still, but now, with their increasing intimacy, something had changed deep inside of her. And now when she looked at him she felt something entirely different. She struggled to find the word that would describe it. The one word she kept coming back to was "dear". His face was dear to her now. She turned away suddenly as the realization slammed into her that she had fallen for him. She swallowed.

"Xander," she finally said. "Before we go, I must ask you one thing."

"Yes?" he asked briefly.

"You say you will never love again, but you will still marry, won't you? To someone you don't love, maybe. But you will still marry?"

"Of course", he said.

"Then, maybe," she said with her usual emphatic delivery, "we could—" He held up his hand to stop her from talking. But there was no need, her confidence had instantly waned at the expression on his face.

"I think we should leave this place. Now," he said in a cold, authoritative voice. "There's nothing to be gained by staying. We've done what we were going to do."

She gripped her stomach where the pain of his words had landed but he wasn't aware; he didn't turn around. If he'd slapped her around the face she didn't think she could have felt more hurt. And, what did she do when she was hurt? Retreat into coldness, just as he'd done, just as she should have done earlier.

"Of course."

"We'll return to Sharq Havilah where you can stay until we identity the man who threatened you. It should only be a few days. The last report was promising. We're homing in on him."

"I won't be returning to Sharq Havilah. As you say, the threat is almost past. I've run away and hidden long enough. I am queen and I will return to my country from here."

"Are you sure?"

She nodded, suddenly feeling very sure. "Yes. I no longer feel afraid."

"Because we've nearly caught the perpetrator?"

No, she thought, but didn't say. Because you've taken away my fears of men. Because I'm whole again. "Yes, exactly that," she lied.

"Right. I'll leave some of my men here to escort you back to the palace."

She nodded, although she had no intention of allowing them to do so. She had her own plans.

It wasn't long before Xander was on his way. They hadn't spoken again, and she didn't watch him leave. It would have been too painful. Instead, she simply waited. And, when she judged he was long gone, she picked up her phone.

Message after message from her vizier filled the screen. He, at least, was faithful. He was her way forward. She didn't hesitate this time, but pressed the button and spoke her instructions clearly to him.

CHAPTER 10

*E*laheh had dismissed the remaining guards as soon as she knew her vizier was on his way to collect her. With every minute that Xander had gone, her anger had grown—anger that she'd let her guard down and allowed Xander into her heart. Anger that he had rejected it.

She hadn't even known she *had* a heart until Xander had made it his mission to help her. Help her! As if she needed help. She caught her breath as she watched the dust which signaled the departure of Xander and his men, fade.

She turned away. But, of course, she had needed help. And he'd done just that—helped her come to terms with what had happened to her, what had changed the course of her life so many years ago. He'd made her into a new woman who could look forward to a future like any other woman could have.

But, in the process, he'd stolen her heart and tossed it back to her, unwanted, open and hurting.

Her future would have to be faced without Xander by her side, or in her bed. It felt like a long empty gray road to be endured rather than properly lived. At least before Xander had awoken her heart, her life had been filled and made meaningful through duty. But now duty faded into insignificance beside the love which Xander had awoken in her.

Her feelings of utter despair were suddenly arrested by the sound of an engine coming from the other direction. It would be her vizier, come to collect her. She might be alone, but she could be queen to the country she was born to rule, and she could marry and bear children to continue her family's long, proud rule. It still didn't feel enough, but it would. She'd make it work. She was Queen of Tawazun and she *would* make it work. *And*, she thought, if I say it enough to myself, I might just begin to believe it.

As the Range Rover approached, Elaheh focused on the bear-like man who was her vizier. He was the son of her father's vizier but was nothing like his father, who'd been obsequious. Abzari was a proud man and had been a good advisor to her. He'd been alone amongst her advisors in agreeing with her that she shouldn't marry too soon. He'd always supported her and would protect her in these last few hours until the man was found who'd written the threatening letters. Xander, himself, had said that they should know by the end of the day. By the time she'd reached her country and palace all would be out in the open and she'd be safe. Alone, maybe, but safe.

"Your Highness," the vizier greeted her.

"Abzari," she said, pleased to see his familiar face after a week away. "It's good to see you."

Did she imagine it, or was his expression different?

Reminiscent of her father's—aloof, disapproving and... what was that? Something simmering behind his eyes. Could it be anger? Then he appeared to collect himself and the usual impassive, mannered expression settled back onto his face.

"I'm glad to see you well, Your Highness. I... we were all so concerned."

"There was no need," she said, turning away to collect her personal things. "I told you on the video call that I was safe."

"But you didn't say what the issue was."

She shot him a sharp look. "No, I didn't." And she had no intention of saying anything to him about it. She looked away. "Now, maybe we can get on our way." She looked around the tent and tried not to think of what she'd found here. Fleeting happiness in the arms of a man who was indifferent to her.

"Of course, my queen. I took the liberty of providing you some refreshments for the journey."

"You think I was lacking in refreshment here?" She sighed heavily. "So be it, if it makes you happy and we can get on our way." Really, she didn't know why Abzari was fussing so, but at least someone was. She downed the glass in one and handed it back to him. "Now, perhaps we can proceed."

She climbed into the back of the Range Rover and settled her robes around her, noting that cushions had been added. Again, it seemed Abzari was determined to make her feel comfortable on the short journey back to her country.

"Settle back, my queen," he said, their eyes meeting in

the rear view mirror. "And I will return you to where you belong."

She sighed as a peculiar languor swept over her. Suddenly the cushions seemed more inviting.

"Maybe," she murmured. She rested her head against the cushion and felt herself slide to one side. She felt too tired to be surprised as the light faded quickly and she fell into a dreamless sleep where not even Xander could reach her.

"WHAT THE HELL ARE YOU DOING?" Xander lifted up his sunglasses and eyed the men he'd told to stay with Elaheh. "I told you to stay with her until I gave word!"

The men muttered and looked askance, not willing to say that they took the word of a woman over Xander.

He stood with his hands on his hips, surveying his men. "Don't tell me. I know. I suppose she dismissed you and you had no choice."

The men nodded, and muttered again. Xander turned away, exasperated. That woman! Why couldn't she do as he wanted for once? He gnawed his lip, still with his back to his men. He didn't want them to see exactly how concerned he was by the thought of her alone, in the desert, with only a few domestic staff for company until her own staff arrived.

He'd assumed she would do as he'd suggested and wait until she'd heard for sure about the identity of the letter writer and only then return home. But, now he thought back, he realized she'd never said she agreed. He'd made that assumption.

And, it seemed after a quick call to the skeleton

domestic staff who'd remained to care for her, there had been only one person turn up to meet her—not her usual security team. And, they hadn't set off in the direction of Tawazun but had turned, deeper into the desert, toward the Empty Quarter.

What was she playing at? Maybe she'd asked her vizier to take her somewhere more secure, away from everyone else? Who knew with Ela?

He fidgeted with the car keys in his pocket, intuition desperately wanting him to return to Ela. This was ridiculous. She was a grown woman who could look after herself. But still the thought of her—eyes opened wide, her mouth breathing his name as she responded to his intimate touch, her soul and heart hurt by the past—shot into his mind's eye. He had to know she was okay. There was no way he could return home until he knew she was safe.

"Your Highness!" One of his men held out his phone. "News from the palace!"

Xander had no idea what kind of news but he had a feeling it wouldn't be good.

He took the phone. "Yes?"

"It's the Grand Vizier of Tawazun, Your Highness," said one of his security team that he'd tasked with finding out the identity of the letter writer. "We've had a breakthrough. It seems he'd got sloppy as he'd become more desperate to find her."

"What are you talking about? What has the grand vizier to do with the stalker?"

"Everything, sir. He *is* the stalker. Abzari wrote those threatening letters."

Xander felt the blood rush from his face as he swore under his breath. "Does she know yet?"

"No, sir. You instructed me to come direct to you with any news."

"Good," said Xander, his brain racing through the different scenarios. If Elaheh didn't know, her Grand Vizier wouldn't know he was on to him. It gave him a slight advantage. He finished the call and issued new commands. There was no way he was risking Elaheh's life by doing what he wanted—go after her alone and wrest her from her vizier. He needed back-up; he needed whatever it took to make sure Ela was safe.

He turned around his vehicle and, with a convoy of security cars following, retraced his steps, but not towards the castle, toward the Empty Quarter, toward the place where Elaheh had last been seen heading.

THE FIRST TIME SHE AWOKE, the world revealed itself to Ela in out-of-focus freeze frames, one after another—disjointed and confusing. She had no idea where she was, or whether she was dreaming. In the end she closed her eyes and drifted away into unconsciousness again.

The second time she awoke her vision focused more quickly on a man seated the other side of a fire, his face familiar through the lick of solid orange flames. His eyes were fixed on her.

"Abzari! What's happening? Where are we?"

"The place where you feel most at home, Elaheh. The desert, where we both belong."

The one thing that instantly struck her was the use of

her first name. He'd never called her by her name. And that he should now sent a deep stab of fear into her gut.

She rose unsteadily to her feet, and clutched her head, which throbbed with a headache the like of which she'd never before experienced.

"Why…" Then she looked at him again, and realized what he'd done. "What was in that drink you gave me?"

He rose and came over to her. The fire crackled and popped next to them. "Something to make it easier for you to have what it is you want."

She shook her throbbing head. "What are you talking about? What the hell is going on, Abzari? Why did you drug me? Why did you bring me here?" She looked around into the darkness which had descended while she'd been in her own personal darkness. "And where are we anyway?"

"That doesn't matter. What does matter, Elaheh, is that we are together at last, without people who could interrupt us."

Before she could reply he took her hands in his—his hands which had never dared touch her before—and jerked her, not farther away, but closer to him. She collided with his chest and could smell the cloying scent he used, and for an instant she thought how different the smell of Xander was. Xander she wanted to inhale totally, but the smell of Abzari made her gag.

"What do you think you are doing? I repeat, take your hands off me immediately."

His lip curled, and he shook its head. "No. You're not going to get away from me again."

"It was you, wasn't it? You are the person who left the notes."

"Of course. Who else loves you like I do? You didn't even consider it would be me, did you? You and your family have always been so superior. But I have always been there for you. Your future is with me, by my side."

Elaheh had to fight the fear which threatened to turn her legs to jelly. Think, she said to herself, think. "Of course, you're right. You have always been there for me. But, what I don't understand, is why you had to write to me. Why the notes? Why not simply tell me how you felt?"

"It wasn't that easy. You saw me only as your vizier. I wanted you to see me as a man who wanted you for your purity, someone who would do anything for you."

"I don't want you to do anything for me. All I want is for you to work for me, as you have been doing. Nothing more."

"Work?" His hold on her wrists tightened. "Is that all you want me for? I will show you there is more to me than that."

He pulled her to him and she felt his breath on her face. Her breathing was coming fast. She felt like a trapped bird. All it would take would be for him to flex his hand and she felt as if she would snap.

Then he frowned, and shook his head. "Don't be afraid, Elaheh." She blanched. "It will be beautiful, and then, after, you will be mine, and you will come to love me as I love you."

She stepped away, taking advantage of him letting her go. "You forget yourself, Abzari."

His frown lifted. "No, you're wrong. For the first time in a long time, I remember myself. I have been your family's greatest supporter for years and now it's time for payback."

"I didn't think you worked in order to receive payback. You think I owe you something?"

"I *know* you do."

With every statement she took a step back, her mind racing for a way to get away from her vizier, and back to safety. But then her heels slammed against the wall of a crumbling hut and she realized she had nowhere else she could move. Xander... The name echoed in her brain, taunting her. He'd told her stay where she was until he contacted her. He'd held her safe until she'd driven him away. But Xander couldn't save her now. He had no idea where she was and no doubt he was safely back in his own palace. But his name might save her.

She tilted up her head. "And what, Abzari, do you consider I owe you?"

He stepped closer again, his palms pressed against the crumbling adobe walls, either side of her shoulders. She was trapped. His angry, intelligent eyes were changed by lust. She at least could recognize now when a man was aroused.

"You," he said, his full lips forming the shape of a kiss.

She slammed her hand against his chest as he tried to take that kiss from her. "Stop right there! What can you possibly hope to gain by attacking me, your queen?"

He frowned, as if hurt. "Attacking? I'm not attacking you." Then the frown vanished, replaced by a leer. "I'm about to make love to you."

Even while inside she reeled in terror, her mind worked overtime. Think. Think. "And then what? Have you stopped to consider what I will do when we return? Do you really expect to get away with this?" She stopped suddenly, realizing that he couldn't possibly expect to get away with it, in which case he must believe that she'd never return to her country, never see anyone—never see Xander again. She bit her lip trying to stop them trembling as terror filled her.

"Of course. Because you will be carrying my child—heir to Tawazun. My heir. You would be too shamed to admit what had happened to you. No, we will marry and I will take my rightful place by your side." He gripped her shoulder. "I know you are scared because you are pure, but you will soon get used to it."

"I am not scared, because this will not happen!" Tears streamed down her face, betraying her fear.

"Yes, it will." Without waiting for her to reply, he pressed his lips against hers and lifted her robes.

She screamed and pulled away. "Stop this madness immediately, Abzari!"

"It is not madness! You will be mine! I will be the first and only one to have you."

"No! You won't be!"

He gripped her chin, but at least pulled away from the kiss. "What do you mean?"

"I mean that the King of Sharq Havilah and myself have decided to marry."

"No."

The one single word hung between them.

"You are pure," he continued. "No one can appreciate you as I do."

"I am pure no longer."

"What do you mean?"

She took a deep breath to tell the lie. "I mean that Xander and I have made love."

"No. That's wrong. I do not believe you would dishonor me like that."

She suddenly realized he was completely crazy. Somewhere in the depths of his twisted mind, he'd always believed they would be together.

She shook her head in disbelief.

"No," he repeated. "You are still pure. You are merely saying that to try put me off you." He pushed his fingers through her hair and his fingers gripped her until her eyes watered. "You won't put me off you, Elaheh. No matter what you say."

"He'll be coming here for me. You can't do this, Abzari."

He grunted. "You're bluffing. No one knows we are here. And no one will know. I intend to stay here until you are carrying our baby. Only then will we return to marry."

The color drained from her face and she felt sick and weak, as she realized that he could carry his plan out. He kicked open the door to the hut and pulled her inside. One glance told her the tumbledown place had been furnished, and was well stocked with supplies for at least a month—long enough for him to carry out his plans.

"Now, get on the bed!"

And in that moment she realized there was nothing she could do. Nothing, except fight—with her body and her mind. And she would go on fighting while she had a breath left in her body.

XANDER DROVE with his foot slammed flat on the floor, urging the vehicle to go ever faster, willing the increasing wind not to cover over the tire prints of the car which had preceded him. He'd left his lands, and those of Tawazun, behind him now and had entered the vast edges of the red deserts of the Rub' Al Khali, or the Empty Quarter as the Europeans had so prosaically called it. Thousands of years ago, the caravans of the Frankincense trade were able to cross these lands. But now they were drier and far more inhospitable than they had been before and few tribes inhabited the area. If the sands shifted, covering the tracks, Xander knew he didn't stand a hope in hell of finding Ela.

He continued on as the sky darkened, but showed no stars—a sign that they were in for bad weather. Then he blinked, and he realized that the tracks had disappeared. He stopped the car and for a moment despair filled him. He stepped outside, pushed up his sunglasses and stared all around at the light which was deepening like a bruise, crushed by the elements, discolored by the oncoming storm.

"Ela!" He called out to the dumb wilderness of orange sands and black clouds. "Ela!" he called again, before pressing his hands to his temples in near despair. He twisted first one way and then another, searching the thickening gloom for signs of life. Behind him he knew his people would be following. But it was in front of him he strained his eyes, looking for anything out of the ordinary, anything which would reveal her whereabouts.

It wasn't until he returned to the car, out of the sand-whipped air, and pulled out a map, that he knew. No one would venture far in this weather. It would be suicide. And he definitely knew that suicide wasn't the intention of the vizier. His finger moved around the spot he was in until it stopped on a small black dot. And lingered there. It showed a small settlement had once existed there—maybe still was there for all he knew. He got onto the old-fashioned communication device they used in the desert and briefly told his team where he was headed, and that they should follow. But he couldn't wait for them. Every second counted.

He put his foot down and, holding the compass, headed toward the small point on the map which was his only hope.

"HOW DARE you speak to me like that?" Elaheh decided fighting with her wits was most likely to be effective. "I am your queen."

He shook his head. "Once, maybe. But now you are the woman I love and intend to make my wife."

"Love? Love?" she repeated, incredulous. "Is this how you treat someone you love?"

He took a step toward her and she had to fight not to step away. To do that would be to show weakness and she knew that never worked. "It's how I treat someone who I need to claim." He leered at her closely. "And I will make you mine. I'll keep you here for as long as it takes to make you pregnant. And then you would be too humiliated to do anything other than make me your husband."

"You are wrong."

"No, I'm not wrong. You are too proud for anyone to imagine you have been humbled as I intend to humble you."

Think, Elaheh, think. She had only her brains to protect her now. He was too big and too strong and she wasn't trained in self defense to handle him. The only way out was the car and he had the keys in his pocket.

"You're right, of course, Abzari," she said, forcing her voice low and submissive.

His frown lifted and a sickening smile spread over his face. "I knew you'd see reason." He gripped her shoulder and pulled her to him. It was what she wanted but she still had to force herself not to be repelled by everything about him—his sweating body, his odor, and the forceful grip of him. "Now, kiss me."

That was going too far. She knew she couldn't do it without retching. She tried to smile but his mouth was open on hers, open and wet, his tongue pushing into her mouth. She cried out, as at the same time her hand groped him, trying to find the keys. He seemed to take this as encouragement and pressed his hard erection against her, his hands bunching up her skirts, trying to draw them up her legs.

Just as his bear-like hands gripped her naked thigh she found the keys, pulled away from him and with all the force she could muster, kneed him in the groin. He doubled up with an oomph of air and an agonizing cry.

She ran around toward the door, yanked it open and then made a mistake. She turned to him, still bent double.

"I am not too proud to protect myself… in any way I can," she said between gritted teeth. But, to her horror, he roared and threw himself at her and knocked her against the adobe wall, her head striking it and making the world spin. He slapped her face with his open hand and she tasted the metallic tang of blood, as the room turned upside down and she fell to the floor.

Elaheh lay on the beaten earth floor and spat blood

out from her mouth. Her cheek pounded where he'd hit her. A roar filled her ears. At first she'd thought it was the blood pounding in her confused head, combined with the frenzied roar of Abzari. It was only when the table exploded into splinters as Abzari's body fell onto it, that she realized, in her confusion that there was someone else in the room, someone else who was roaring.

Elaheh tried to roll over to see what was happening but the pain was too much on her arm. Lights suddenly exploded all around her, beaming into the room through previously black windows. She wondered if she'd died and had gone to hell—the pain, the screams and the fiery lights. The thought faded as her world suddenly turned black.

CHAPTER 11

"Ela, Ela," the gentle voice repeated, over and over. She was reminded of her mother, not least because she felt as if she were being rocked to sleep, the gentle touch of a hand upon her cheek. Perhaps it wasn't hell she'd landed in, but heaven. A promised land where she could forget her pain and sorrows and be reunited with her mother.

She sighed and tried to turn over but a blast of pain shot through her. No, not heaven then. This was the pain of the living. She opened her eyes to find Xander's tender gaze upon her.

"Thank God you've awoken."

She struggled to sit up but winced as they were thrown around.

"We're just leaving the desert, there's an ambulance waiting. Sit back. Your arm is broken."

She did as he said, finding his own arm was cradling her. He held her against him, softening the bouncing of the vehicle, and she turned her face to his body, needing his comfort, as his hand stroked over her back.

"I have you now, Ela. I have you. You're safe."

She didn't want to move, but she had to know. With all the effort she could, she looked up at him. "What about Abzari? What happened to him?"

"He's dead. Killed by his own hand rather than face the consequences of his actions. He had a knife on him but he turned it on himself, rather than me, or you."

She closed her eyes briefly as the image of self-inflicted violence slammed into her mind. "I don't know what happened to him. For years he watched out for me, protected me. And all the while…" She couldn't bear to express what it was she now knew he'd been thinking.

"All the while he was hiding his true thoughts and feelings. He wanted you, and he wanted your kingdom. And he was determined to have both, no matter what it took."

"You know, he might have succeeded, if it weren't for you, Xander."

"I came along just in time."

"No." She held her finger against his cheek. "I don't mean that. I mean that you taught me how to be strong."

"You were always strong."

She shook her head. "Not inside. Inside I was scared, and you took away that fear. That was why I could stand up to him. That was what delayed him from raping me."

"Enough time for me to come for you."

She nodded. "Without that strength I found in myself, things could have been very different."

The vehicle suddenly stopped and the flashing lights of the ambulance filled the car. Ela looked out the window and recognized the road. It was the junction between her country and Xander's.

Xander jumped out, opened her door and carried her to the ambulance. But she insisted on standing, on stepping up into the ambulance under her own power, despite the pain.

Xander shouted orders to the ambulance driver. "Sharq Havilah Hospital! As fast as you can."

"No!" Elaheh's voice was quiet but commanding. Everyone turned to her. "No. I wish to return to my country," she said, looking at Xander. Then she turned to the ambulance driver. "Tawazun, please. The palace. Have the medical team meet me there."

As she was settled into the back of the ambulance, Xander gripped the door and watched. It was only when she and the nurses had settled that he spoke.

"Tawazun?" he asked, in disbelief.

She nodded. "I'm Queen of Tawazun and I will return there. I'll not cower or hide from anyone, ever again. I'll stand on my own two feet from now on."

"But why?"

"Because you showed me I could."

Xander stepped away, the ambulance lights alternately slicing his face with blood-red and a yellow-gray—both were distorting, both revealed a pain which had Elaheh sitting up, beginning to reach out for him, changing her mind. But, before she could, the doors slammed shut and Xander disappeared from view.

As they drove away she closed her eyes and imagined Xander watching her leave. He'd saved her, he had feelings for her, she knew that. But, ultimately, they had no future. They were both leaders of their respective countries and duty had to come first. If he'd loved her, it might have been different, but he'd made it clear that his heart was buried in the desert alongside the woman he'd loved so many years before. And Xander had awoken in her a heart which needed to be loved and wouldn't settle for anything less.

~

IT HAD TAKEN only months for Elaheh's physical wounds to heal, but she was still waiting for the emotional pain of her separation from Xander to heal. Some days it was deadened by the constant work and pressure she put herself under as she continued to work hard as leader of her country. Other days—especially at night—the pain was keen like a freshly made knife wound and at those times she despaired.

Last night had been one of those nights. She'd dreamed of him caressing and kissing her, teasing her with his lips and his fingers, and when she'd awoken to an empty bed, breathless with lust, the pain of her loss hit her more sharply than ever.

She rose from her desk, unable to focus.

She knew she loved him, and that he was still in love with a girl who'd died years earlier. But she also knew she was stronger now than she'd ever been; she was a woman able to ask for what she wanted.

She'd worked hard to strengthen her country so it was able to move forward into a future of economic and cultural strength. She'd appointed new advisors who were keen to see Tawazun become the powerful nation it had the potential to be, but had also worked with established figures who would ensure their country's past wasn't forgotten. If she could do that successfully, she could do anything. *Anything.* The word echoed in her brain. Maybe even marry a man she loved with all her heart, but who didn't love her.

When she'd been driven away from him that night in the ambulance, she'd lied to Xander, and to herself. She'd told him that duty had to come first—her duty to her country. But it had been an excuse. What had come first was her pride. She didn't want to admit she loved someone who didn't love her.

But the intervening months had shown her the truth of that old adage, pride comes before a fall. Because while her status as queen and her country had gone from strength to strength, her heart and emotions had been in free fall, and it was only when they'd landed that she knew she couldn't continue without him. Or at least, she couldn't continue without asking him for what she wanted. It was her last chance at happiness.

She jumped up and called her assistant. She refused to have another night dreaming of what she wanted, without asking for it. If he said no, she'd move on. Life would never be quite as she wanted it, but she'd make it into something. And... there was a chance he might say yes. And then what a life awaited her! Her heart quickened at the thought. She was determined to use any weapon she had to full advantage. If she had to seduce him first, then she would. Seduce and then propose. It was a daunting plan, but she was no longer a woman to be daunted by anything.

~

LIFE FELT like food devoid of flavor since Xander had left Ela. He'd taken little nibbles of it for sustenance, but had soon been put off by its dryness and tastelessness. He wanted fire but there was none to be had anywhere else.

He'd spent the intervening months watching Ela grow in queenship from afar, leading her country on to great things. The video meetings between the leaders of their countries were impersonal things, business-like and brief. He'd barely exchanged half a dozen words with Ela, and they'd been strictly business. The work they'd done earlier on the infrastructure project had been completed and handed on to their administrators. There was no reason for them to be alone together anymore, despite Xander racking his brains, trying to conjure up a reason.

No, Ela no longer needed him. She'd moved on. But had he?

He pushed himself off the chair reluctantly and walked over to the window, and looked out at the darkening sky streaked with apricot from the sun which had slipped behind the indigo horizon. The city which lay before him, and the land which stretched to the blue-hazed mountains, was no longer something to be avoided, something thrust upon him by Roshan. Ever since the massacre of his parents and beloved Selya, he'd hated the place. But hate was the flip side to love and, it seemed, at some point over the past months, his life had done a 180 and landed squarely on the side of love again. And who had brought about that change? One person who'd reached into his heart, squeezed it, shaken it about it a bit, and, in so doing, had resuscitated it.

Absent-mindedly he rubbed his chest, where his heart beat with a life which was more than the physical pumping supply of blood around his body. This new heart of his affected everything he did—from his interactions with his people, to his decisions about their welfare, to his love for his brother and his growing family. But this new heart of his also felt pain now. Especially at night, when he had nothing to fill his mind, no busyness to occupy his thoughts. Then, like now, the absence of the woman he loved, and who no longer needed him, crept into every corner of his being, poking his newly found sensitivity, and finding it raw and needy.

He closed his eyes against the sea breeze which had quickened as the sun had set and imagined her voice. Even from the beginning he'd enjoyed listening to her. He smiled to himself as he remembered how much she'd irritated him. But now he knew that the irritation was because even then, she'd hit that place he'd protected so keenly.

He closed his eyes even more tightly as he imagined her saying his name, as she climaxed in his arms. It aroused him like nothing else. He didn't know why he taunted himself. But he couldn't help himself.

Then he heard his name again. Her soft, breathy, sultry tones seemed more real somehow. He shook his head and gripped the edge of the window, willing himself to accept reality, to banish the voice from his brain. But it came again. Closer this time. He opened his eyes wide and turned around.

Ela stood before him in all her imperious beauty, her lips still open from having spoken his name. He didn't move. Was he really going mad? Had his desperate need for her summoned up her image, too?

"Xander." She smiled. "Aren't you going to say something? Even if it's to ask how I managed to persuade your guards to allow me entry?"

If she'd only said his name, he would still have doubted his sanity and her reality. But the fact that she spoke and stepped closer toward him banished the last ideas that he was living a dream. But there was only one way to be certain.

He stepped forward and took hold of her outstretched hands in his own and squeezed them tight. "Ela! Is it really you?"

"Of course it is. Unless there's an Elaheh impersonator somewhere who has equal powers of persuasion with your guards."

He brought her hands to his lips and kissed them. Then he sighed and allowed his gaze to rove over her lovely features. "I was just thinking of you."

Her face, which had worn an almost hesitant expression, broke out into a big smile. "Really? Nothing bad I hope."

He shook his head. "No, nothing bad. I was just imagining…" He faltered, unwilling to tell her the exact directions of his thoughts.

"Just imagining… what?"

If he told her and she was merely here to finalize some matter of state he'd forgotten, he'd look a fool. He needed to know.

"Ela, why are you here?"

Her gaze faltered and she licked her lips, opened her mouth, closed it, and then looked up at him with a firm smile as if forcing herself forward. "I'm here because you never gave me something I wanted."

He frowned. "I didn't?" His mind raced over what he

possibly had withheld from her. There was nothing that he could think of. He'd even given her his heart, even if she didn't know it.

"No."

"And what was that?"

He hadn't realized that watching a woman swallow nervously could be so alluring.

"You didn't make love to me."

And with those words his world tilted on its axis, finding a firmer footing.

"Ah. So you don't call it sex anymore."

"No. Maybe with other people—"

A blast of jealous anger shot through his body. It must have shown in his expression because she moved closer to him, brushing her hand across his chest before looking up to him once more, her lips close to his body.

"Not that I've tried with other people, because I'm not interested in sex. Only making love. Only with you," she added in an undertone.

Xander hadn't realized he was holding such a tight knot inside of him. He must have grown accustomed to it and now only knew it was there when it relaxed, as if Ela had plucked away the knot of an elaborate silky bow and it had slithered away to the ground, leaving him free for the first time in forever.

"Is that right?" he said, slipping his hands around her waist. "And why, Ela, have you decided to wait this long before asking me again?"

She pouted and it was all he could do not to press his lips against those full sensual lips immediately. But he wanted to know her answer.

"I asked you once before and you refused."

"And yet you've come again. I wonder why. I wonder what's changed."

"Me. I have."

Her words were simple, but their meaning was anything but. He needed to know. "In what way?"

She was less sure now. Her eyelids flickered as her mind raced, trying to put her thoughts into words. "You asked me once to surrender myself to you."

"Yes, but—" But before he could explain, she'd placed a finger against his lips.

"I know you didn't mean it any demeaning way. But you're right. My pride had gotten in the way, and I suddenly realized what you meant. I had to let go of all the stupid things which were stopping me from coming to you with an open heart." She looked into his eyes with one steady stare. "I had to let go of my pride because, in the end, it was the only thing which lay between me and you." She raised her other hand and pressed it against his chest, spreading her fingers. He could feel their heat. "And I do want you, Xander."

It took all his self-control not to pick her up in his arms and carry her to the bed and make love to her very, very thoroughly. Instead, he pulled away a little, looked down at her. "Then prove it," he said with a barely suppressed growl.

It was her turn to frown. "How? Tell me how, and I will."

"I've listened to your words, now I need to feel what your body will tell me. Only then will I truly believe you."

The frown disappeared into a brief twist of a smile before she raised herself onto tiptoe and she pressed those beautiful lips against his. She moved away all too soon.

He clenched his hands tight to stop himself from responding. He wanted to grab her, throw her on the bed, rip off her underwear and thrust himself deep inside of her. But such an aggressive approach was all wrong with Elaheh. He had to take his time. Maybe later their love-making would develop, but now, she had to take the lead.

"Over to you, Ela," he said in a soft whisper.

Elaheh felt Xander's words give her a strength, flowing through her body, lighting up every part with desire and confidence. She stepped away, amused by the faint traces of uncertainty in Xander's eyes. He didn't know what she was about to do. Good. It made her even more certain that she could trust her instincts, the same way she could trust her brain.

She shrugged off her abaya and tossed it to the floor. She only had a vague feeling of discomfort. Usually she made sure it was folded, and handed to a servant to put away or wash. Nothing was ever left on the ground in a crumpled heap. She found crossing this threshold liberating.

With renewed purpose she disposed of the short silk dress she wore beneath her robes in the same way.

Xander went and flicked off the light. All that was left was the slices of moonlight across the floor, leading to the bed. Not enough for her. She wanted to see, she wanted to experience everything.

"No, leave the light on. I want to see you. And I want you to see me."

He grinned. "Sure." He flicked the light back on. "Now," he gestured to her. "Please, continue."

She was pleased she'd had the foresight to wear a bra which clipped in the front. With one twist of her fingers she was free of it and tossed it on top of her other clothes. No need, really, to spread her clothes too far and wide. And then she stepped out of her panties and tossed them to one side. She had no idea if she looked good to his eyes. She'd heard of other women shaving in private areas for their men, of making their nipples redder, of adorning their private parts with jewels. She'd done none of that. There was only herself, and she hoped that would be enough.

It seems from his reaction, that it was. "Um, perfection," he said, as he walked up to her and cupped her cheeks and kissed her thoroughly.

She hadn't anticipated how erotic it would be, standing before the man she loved and desired more than anyone on the planet, naked and vulnerable, and yet powerful at the same time.

She rolled back on to her heels once more. There was only one thing she could think of that would be more erotic and that was to see Xander without any clothes on and to press her naked body to his, to feel and know every inch of his body not through her sight, but by the feel of it against her skin.

Her fingers fumbled as she tried to undo first one button on his shirt, and then another. Meanwhile his hands were firm on her bottom, pulling her hips against him, her stomach caressing his erection, making her movements even clumsier. In the end she tore at his clothes, the buttons from his shirt bouncing across the tiled floor. Then she could wait no more and pressed her lips to his chest and then stomach as her fingers busied themselves opening his trousers and releasing his erection into her waiting hands.

She knew exactly what she wanted to do first. With his hard flesh between her hands, she looked up into his eyes so he could see her reaction, lifted herself onto her toes, extending herself as tall as possible so she could give herself the pleasure for which she yearned. Then she rubbed herself against him. She gasped at the first touch, tilted her head back with a sigh as she moved his moist tip around her most sensitive of places, and then felt desire drain her strength as she relaxed into his hands.

With one swift movement he lifted her into his arms and she wrapped her legs around his waist, kissing him with a passion she hadn't known existed inside her. She wanted everything he could give her now.

He sat on the bed as she rose on her knees to allow him better access to her breasts which he took—first one and then the other—into his mouth, suckling her, sending her nipple, hard and needy, deeper into his mouth, tugging at some invisible cord deep inside her.

At the same time he explored her sex with his fingers. She was wetter than she'd ever been and wanted him now. She didn't want to wait another moment for him to be inside of her.

She tried to push him back onto the bed but he wouldn't budge. It seemed her willpower had met its match.

He looked up from his attention to her breasts, grinned and swiftly twisted her around until she was flat on her back on the bed. He tried to reach for a condom but she stopped him. "Not necessary," she gasped, and grabbed him again to make sure he wasn't going anywhere. If he'd had any thought of stopping, it had disappeared as she touched him.

Focusing on his eyes, holding his gaze, she opened her legs wide. For a moment she felt exposed, uncomfortable, too far from her comfort zone of absolute proprietary. But she forgot all her worries when she saw how turned on he was.

He lifted her legs and kissed her sex. The touch made her tremble with anticipation. She thrust her fingers through his hair and gripped it as he tasted her. It only took her seconds for the sensations to escalate into a powerful orgasm which rocked her and left her body reeling.

But she had no time to luxuriate in the feelings, as Xander positioned himself and with one swift, slick movement entered her. For a second she was shocked by how deeply he'd penetrated her. And she tensed.

He didn't move, just kept himself there, as he bypassed her fears by playing with her nipples with his tongue before kissing her as deeply and as intently as he was inside of her.

She relaxed under his ministrations, and he felt it, and only then slipped out of her, the sensations as his skin moved against hers sending waves of pleasure through her body to the tips of her toes.

"Oh," she breathed with surprise. She gripped his bottom, worried he was going to come out, but then he pushed back, still gently, and any other thought or worry was swept away by the explosion of sensation that filled her.

Back and forth he went, pulling out and then pushing back in again. Each time, her senses ratcheted up a notch. She felt as if she were pushed to the edge of a pool of deep, sweet water, after years of drought. All she wanted was to fall into it and drown in pleasure. But Xander wasn't in any rush, and was determined to make sure the journey to surrender was equally pleasurable. Ela might have initiated the love-making, but Xander was making sure he remained aware of every nuance or suggestion of feeling from Ela, so pleasure was her only response.

Only then, when he had no doubts, did he release his self-control enough to replace the gentleness with a more assertive passion which Ela fully appreciated.

They both came at the same time, Ela clinging on to his shoulders as he pumped with his hips—short, sharp movements—all that he had into her. In that moment she knew she couldn't live without this. And that she'd do anything—anything—to make him hers.

He rolled onto his side and pulled her hard against him, enveloped her in his arms and kissed her. Then they both fell into a half-sleep or daze—she couldn't have described it. She didn't know how long it lasted. But when she came to, he was still holding her and her legs were sticky with his seed. Tentatively she touched it, and he groaned and replaced her finger with his own. She rolled onto her back, helpless under the onslaught of his clever touch.

The evening turned into night—a night of lovemaking and snatched sleep—and the night turned into day once more. It was the same, Elaheh mused as she lay, their legs tangled, her mind and body totally relaxed—as one, and yet totally different.

She swung her legs onto the floor and went to the

bathroom. By the time she emerged from the shower, she was dressed.

Xander turned to her sleepily. It didn't look as if he'd moved.

"You're up early," he said, sitting up.

"And I ordered coffee." She placed a cup beside the bed.

"Hm," he said, taking a sip of the hot, strong liquid. "I take it you're moving on," he said with wry grin.

She shot him an answering grin. "You know me so well."

"Certainly better than this time yesterday."

Didn't she know it. The delicious soreness between her legs told her so. She nodded. "And," she said slowly, "do you like what you know?"

He reached out and took her hand, kissing it. "I think you know I do."

She nodded again. "I just wanted to be sure before proceeding to the next step."

His grin faded, replaced by a frown. He put down the coffee, rose and put on his robe. He folded his arms and looked at her. "The next step, Ela?"

"Yes, the next step, Xander. It's time to get down to business."

CHAPTER 12

"What?" asked Xander in disbelief. "Ela! What are you talking about?"

"Business, Xander. It's time to move onto business."

Had he really ever believed Ela could change? Xander shook his head in disbelief. He'd just had the best love-making he'd ever experienced and all Ela could do was to say it's time to get down to business.

"You are truly incredible!"

She frowned. "It doesn't sound as if you mean that in a good way."

"In this instance, you're correct, I don't. Tell me, why the hell did you come here anyway? Because it doesn't sound as if you came to make love."

"I came here," she said as if she were a school teacher explaining an obvious fact to her school children, "to show you that we weren't incompatible. In bed, or out," she added, as an afterthought.

Xander could hardly believe his ears. "*Not* incompatible?" he repeated.

181

"Exactly. And I think you have to conclude that we're not."

He shook his head. Was he really hearing these things? But then, of course, this was Ela. "Not what? I think I've lost the thread here."

She cleared her throat, looking more and more uncomfortable with each passing moment.

"Not incompatible," came the whisper. "Maybe I'm not explaining myself very well."

He snorted. "You think? Why don't you just come straight out and say what's on your mind?"

She held up her hand. "Okay. What I'm trying to say is that I think we should get married."

He opened his eyes wide, and he suspected his mouth had followed suit.

"Ela! You never cease to amaze me. One minute you're talking—in a very luke-warm way, I have to say—about how compatible we are, and the next you're saying we should get married. How did you jump from one to the other?"

"Logic."

"Logic?"

She looked positively nervous now, as if she wanted him to rescue her from the mess she'd made of the conversation. Well, he was too riled up to give her a helping hand back into the sanity of his world.

"Yes, logic. Xander. We are no longer enemies. Would you agree?"

He nodded. "Yes," he said slowly.

"Good. We agree on that, at least. You don't even get on my nerves any more," she said, with a disarming grin.

"And you don't get on my nerves any more."

Her grin dropped and her face becoming momentarily frosty. He smiled and she became frostier.

"I don't see how I could get on your nerves," she said.

"You brought up the subject."

The frostiness melted and she nodded. "I suppose I did. Yes, we can talk to each other now without wanting to kill each other. I think that's as good a basis for marriage as anything else."

If it hadn't been for her naive smile he would have thrown a jug of water over her.

"And you think that not wanting to kill each other is a good reason to marry?"

She shrugged. "Of course, why not?" She threw her hands open in an expansive gesture. "After all, our countries will be stronger together than apart. The infrastructure project won't have any of the pitfalls and problems if we are united."

He narrowed his eyes. "We will still be two separate countries."

"Yes, but we are the same people essentially. It's just in my country we are still in touch with our culture."

His face darkened a little. "Meaning we are not?"

She shrugged. "Not exactly." She sighed. "I simply mean that your... " She hesitated while she carefully selected the right word. Xander couldn't help wondering what the words were that she was rejecting. "Your *focus* has been on the economy. By marrying we would unite our countries—not formally—but in practice to be the best of both worlds. Both countries would have all the advantages increased commerce would bring. But the traditional life of your people and mine will continue. If we stand as one we can ensure that this happens."

His arms were still crossed. He felt his frown was a permanent fixture. "That was quite some speech."

"Xander, don't you see? You're single, I'm single, we… like each other, and I enjoyed making love with you. So…"

"So, you think we should marry based on those things."

"Yes, that's right. You would, of course, remain King of Sharq Havilah, and I would—"

"Of course—" he interjected.

She nodded in agreement. "Of course, remain Queen of Tawazun. We would spend half the time in each country, but in this day and age there's nothing to prevent us from continuing to work away from our countries."

He put his hands on his hips. "You appear to have it all worked out."

The nerves vanished and she smiled. "Yes, I've been giving it some thought."

"Excellent," he said between gritted teeth. "Sounds like you arrived here with an agenda. You've at least got one item ticked off it. Sex. Sorry, making love. Any action points I need to know about?"

She licked her lips. "Only…"

"Only?"

"Only when our next meeting will be."

"Our next meeting. Our wedding, perhaps?"

Her face brightened. "Yes, it could be."

His face grew darker. "No, it couldn't," he growled.

"But, Xander! Just think about it. It all makes sense."

"Not to me it doesn't. You're thinking of marriage as you used to think of sex. Simple, uncomplicated copulating. You don't believe that any more, do you?"

"No, of course not. You've shown me it's much more."

He took a step closer to her. "Then use that fierce, logical mind of yours, Ela, to explain to me what it is that makes it much more."

She opened her mouth and then closed it again. Then she took a deep breath and tilted her chin stubbornly upward. "It's how we feel, of course. Our feelings. If you need to know, Xander, then I'll tell you. I love you. There, I said it. I didn't mention it before because I thought it might be unacceptable to you."

It was his turn to be silent. That one word could always shut him up. Love. He hadn't, for one minute, imagined she'd say she loved him, because he didn't believe she did. But he didn't doubt her because one thing about Ela, she rarely lied and she always said what she truly believed, even if it sometimes sounded cold and bizarre.

"You love me," he managed to whisper, as if he'd been winded by her declaration.

"Yes," she said, her brow creased as if she were about to cry.

Images flashed through his mind of all those people he'd loved and lost. Especially his parents and Selya. Losing them had changed his life. It had cut out his heart and Ela had replaced it. He was suddenly so full of emotion, he could do nothing but shake his head.

She took a step away. "I'm sorry, I shouldn't have said anything. It's just that, slowly, bit by bit, you healed me, made me realize I could trust a man, and that I wasn't my mother, and would never be. Just as you are nothing like any man I've ever known before. I trust you, Xander."

"How much?"

She frowned. "How much do I trust you?"

He nodded.

"Completely."

"Right." He walked up to her, put his hands firmly around her waist, lifted her up and threw her over his shoulder. She shrieked and made an oomph sound as if winded. At least the talking would stop.

He took her over to the bed and dropped her onto the silk covers which were already in disarray.

She struggled to sit up. He shook his head and lifted her robes. "You didn't have time to dress completely then."

"No, I—" She shrieked again as his fingers made contact with her sex, and she fell back onto the bed of her own volition. "I… was in a rush."

He didn't let up his exploration, lingering where he knew it would have effect. "Rushing is never a good thing, Ela."

"No." She sucked in air between her teeth, scrunched up her eyes and gripped the bedclothes. "No, you're right. It's not."

She was trembling now, and wetter than he'd ever made her. "Now, you said you trusted me?"

She swallowed and nodded.

"Good." He dipped and kissed her before rolling her over onto her stomach. She went easily. He got the feeling he could do anything to her at that point and she'd enjoy it.

He played with her breasts for a moment, before lifting her hips into position, then he thrust into her from behind. She cried out his name in a breathless rush, just as he'd dreamed her doing so many times. It seemed a dream didn't hold a candle to the real thing.

She was everything he needed, everything that obliterated the past and made him only want to move from the present because he knew the future would be twice as good.

She cried out not once, but twice in orgasm as he thrust repeatedly into her, before he pulsed his seed deep inside of her, claiming her for his own. She might be in doubt as to his response, but he would never have had unprotected sex with someone who he wasn't going to marry. He'd tell her, in time. No rush, he told himself.

ELAHEH LAY ON HER BACK, waiting for her heart to calm down, and for her breathing to settle enough to talk. She pressed her palm against her thudding chest and wondered, again, how it was possible for Xander to create such exquisite pleasure in her body. She had no idea, she just wanted to make sure that he never stopped.

She rolled her head around to face him. She opened her mouth to speak but his face took her breath away. He was so handsome, so strong. She traced his cheekbone, highlighted in the light which streamed through the open window, and then slowly pushed her fingers through his hair and rolled on top of him and kissed him. Eventually she pulled away from the kiss, even as her hips wriggled lightly against his.

"We need to talk, Xander," she said.

He grunted, a very sexual grunt which made her wonder if talking wasn't over-rated. "We won't be doing much talking if you keep lying on top of me like that."

As much as she desired him, she desired to ensure her future with him more. So she rolled off him and rose from the bed. She adjusted her dress and stood at the foot of the bed, looking down on him. He really was magnificent in every way. Now all she had to do was make sure he was hers.

"I'd like—"

"No, Ela. You're not getting your way on this occasion."

Suddenly, he jumped out of bed and walked into the adjoining dressing room.

She stood, speechless and aghast. "Xander!" She stumbled after him, filled with a desperate fear that she'd gone too far, and frightened him off. She stood by the door, gripping it for all it was worth to stop herself from flinging herself onto him and begging him to stay. He had his back to her and was rummaging through his desk, tossing things aside.

"Xander!" she repeated. "I'm sorry!"

He frowned at her briefly before continuing to search.

"Xander!" She had no idea what he was looking for but whatever it was, it was obviously something more important than her. Panic filled her. What if she'd overstepped the mark? What if by being her true self, he didn't like what he saw? What if... She couldn't bear to imagine what if... Because if he left her now, she didn't know what she would do without him. Tears sprung into her eyes, teetered on their surface and then rolled in thick drops down her cheek. "Xander," she croaked, her voice full of emotion, leaning heavily against the wall.

He turned around. "Ela! What the hell?" He came and lifted her chin to his. He was distorted through her tears, everything was, her whole world would shatter without him.

"Please, Xander, I need you, I want you, please don't tell me to go."

He brought her hard against his body, his arms wrapped around her, and kissed her face. "Ela, what the hell made you think I wanted you to go?"

She pulled away, her hair mussed, the tears still distorting her vision. "Because you said I wouldn't be getting my way. And what I wanted was for you to marry me. If you don't want that, then we have no future. And" —another onslaught of tears made her sob—"and, I don't think I could bear that."

"Just as well," he said.

She shook her head in confusion as he pulled away from her, and was suddenly on his knees before her.

"What are you doing?"

"Elaheh, what I am doing is getting on my knees to ask you to marry me."

She choked a laugh through her tears as she suddenly saw what her obscured vision had failed to see earlier. He held in his hands a small velvet box, which he flipped open to reveal the largest diamond ring she'd ever seen in her life—and she'd seen a lot.

Still laughing, she fingered the diamond and looked into his eyes, which suddenly looked unsure.

"Why are you laughing?" he asked. "Don't you think I'm serious?"

"I'm laughing," said Ela, "because I'm so relieved. I thought you were going to tell me to go."

"After what we've done here today? After all that we've gone through these past months?"

She nodded, all laughter vanished now. "What we've been through has changed me. But not all of me. You've helped me get rid of my fears around men, and you've helped break down the barrier of pride I put before me and everyone else. I've surrendered those things, but some things I can't change and won't surrender to anyone, not even you."

"And those things are?"

"Me. All those aspects of me, that are me. I can't change, Xander. And I won't change. I am who I am. The lessons I learned from my mother's life and death remain with me. I have to be myself and stand up for myself—always. Those things I will never surrender."

"And nor, my love, would I want you to."

"I will always be bossy, argumentative, possibly even irritating sometimes…" She trailed off. "You said 'love'."

"I did. I called you 'my love', because you are just that." His gaze roved around her face. "My only love, the one person in this world with whom I want to live my life, side by side, country alongside country." He pushed his fingers through her hair, and cupped her face. "I have no wish for anyone to surrender themselves to me, least of all someone as special, as beautiful, as wonderful, as you."

"Wonderful? Truly? But I can be prickly sometimes, and sometimes I talk too much."

"I wouldn't want you any other way. And, I, no doubt, have qualities which may grate on you."

"A few." She grinned. "It doesn't sound like a recipe for a quiet marriage."

"Good," he said, kissing her again. "Because a quiet marriage is the last thing I want. You'll keep me interested like no one has ever done before. And our coming together will always be more explosive and passionate because of it. Without you, I may get silence, but I won't get peace, because I'll be yearning for you, wanting you, dreaming about you. Ela, I can't live without you, and I can't love without you. It's that simple, and it's that complicated. Please, will you marry me?"

All she could do was nod because the tears welled up again. But, it seemed the nod was sufficient because he pushed the ring onto her finger and then he took the words right out of her mouth with yet another kiss.

EPILOGUE

The air was warm and sultry, and the only sound was the shifting of the leaves which grew above the wall and caught the sea breeze, and the whirr of an overhead fan which cooled them on the terrace below. She normally didn't feel the heat but then, she wasn't normally pregnant.

Elaheh drew in a deep breath of fragrant, jasmine-scented air. She must have fallen pregnant that first night. It could have been the first time, or second, or third—it all happened that first night. She wasn't at all surprised. She and Xander just fitted together—not dominating each other or consuming each other, but like puzzle pieces clicking together to form a whole which was far better, far stronger, than the individual piece she was without him. Complete.

She sighed, focused once more on the chess game before her and pushed her queen across the board. Then she hesitated and sat back to think again, her finger remaining on the queen.

"You can always surrender," said Xander.

She shot him a black look. "I never surrender."

Xander grinned, a very sexual grin. "Sometimes you do."

She lifted her chin, in a haughty movement. "Only if I benefit by it."

"You'll benefit by it now." He glanced at his watch. "You'll have time to prepare for Ashley's visit."

Elaheh didn't look up from the board. Despite the fact she now knew for sure that Xander and Ashley felt nothing but friendship for each other, she preferred it if the beautiful English scholar didn't hang out with Xander too often. Particularly while she was feeling so large and ungainly. Elaheh cleared her throat and pretended to look with renewed concentration at the chess pieces.

"Won't you, Ela?" said Xander slowly.

He knew. She could tell by his tone. She looked up and he shook his head.

"There was no reason to send her away, you know," he continued.

"It's just that I thought our mysterious neighbor might benefit by her expertise."

"I'm sure he will. Ashley knows her stuff."

"And she *was* keen."

"I'm not surprised. Few people are allowed into his country to view its architectural treasures since the borders were closed after the last war. And Sheikh Zyir is notoriously difficult. It's a wonder you were able to persuade him to allow her entry."

She blinked lightly, trying, very ineffectively, to hide her response.

"Ela, what did you do?"

"Ah, well, I may have let slip what her other expertise is."

Xander went still. "You didn't!"

Ela looked up at him briefly from behind lowered lashes. "Well, it is her other specialty."

"She's a feminist historian with interests in middle eastern architecture—"

"Especially with regard to the accommodation of women," Elaheh finished.

"I like the way you omit the one word which would have piqued Sheikh Zyir's interest, no doubt."

"Harem?"

"Exactly, harem. Ashley's interest is purely academic, purely feminist. And Zyir's interest is purely practical. It's rumored he's particularly fond of the old ways, particularly when it comes to keeping a harem of women.

Elaheh dismissed his words with her hand. "I doubt that's true." She really hoped it wasn't true. She was beginning to feel guilty now. But she'd met Ashley a few times and she was one very independent, strong women, who, Elaheh was sure, could easily deal with a macho sheikh, no matter how fierce his reputation. "Anyway, I told her to get in touch with me if she needed anything."

"Get in touch with you, not me."

"Yes."

"Why?"

"Because..." She shrugged. "I worry that you might think you made the wrong decision, that you should have asked Ashley to marry you."

"True. Maybe I should. After all, we would have had far fewer arguments."

Elaheh scowled, and stared at the board, determined

to find a winning move, but her mind was filled with visions of Ashley and Xander.

"And she would have let me do whatever I wish."

Elaheh pushed her queen across the board. "Checkmate," she said, sitting back with a grin and taking a sip of her rose water sharbat. The ice cubes clinked as she set it back on the marquetry table and looked across at her opponent.

Xander eyes were focused on the board. Then he shot her the kind of glance which made her heart race, before pushing a piece—she hadn't a clue which, her mind was suddenly off the game—across the board. He settled back. "I think not."

"Not?" she asked weakly.

He shook his head, and his smile was plainly sexual. "Not checkmate."

She frowned and looked back at the board, and realized he was correct. "You got me riled up with all that talk of Ashley. She's so beautiful."

"True." He smiled, and she could see he'd decided to stop teasing her. "But not as beautiful as you—no one is. And I want no one else in my bed, by my side, mother of my children… the list goes on… except you."

She gave a satisfied noise and looked back at the board. "I thought I'd won for a moment."

"No. But I have." Xander got up and stretched.

Elaheh's frown deepened. She couldn't figure out how someone as apparently laid-back as Xander had a brain which worked with such unerring accuracy. She sighed and began to set the pieces up again. "Let's have another game."

"No."

She looked up at him. "Yes, let's have another game." She continued to replace the pieces back on the board.

"No." He leaned over the board, his hands gripping the side of the table, his gaze boring into her. "I have a better idea."

"But I'd really like to—"

With one clean sweep of his hand, the chess pieces went flying.

"Xander!" She was shocked by the abrupt movement.

His eyes narrowed and he extended a hand to her. She didn't hesitate. Sometimes, she'd found it was in her interests to surrender to her sheikh.

They walked quickly into the sitting room where Xander then proceeded to undress Elaheh until she stood naked in front of him. She suddenly felt self-conscious and cradled her pregnant stomach, as she stood beside the chaise.

He dropped to his knees and kissed her stomach, trailing further kisses down until he found his target. She sat on the chaise and he pushed open her legs, made himself comfortable between them and proceeded to give her the most explosive orgasm, making it absolutely clear to her that there was no one else in the world he adored more than Elaheh. And, Elaheh thought, as her body rippled with the aftermath of the explosion, the feeling was entirely mutual.

Buy the next book in the series now!

Taken for the Sheikh's Harem—A powerful sheikh, a feminist academic, and a harem...

Dear Reader,

Oh my! There were times there when I wondered if Xander and Elaheh would overcome their differences. But it's often the case that, when someone is overly standoff-ish, defensive, or aggressive, they're simply scared. And that was true in Elaheh's case. Luckily for her, Xander wanted to understand her. And, in so doing, came to love her, and heal her. He also came to understand and recover from the traumatic incident which scarred his own life.

I hope you enjoyed *Surrender to the Sheikh*. In case you haven't read the other books in the **The Sheikhs of Havilah** series, they are:

The Sheikh's Secret Baby
Bought by the Sheikh
The Sheikh's Forbidden Lover
Surrender to the Sheikh

Taken for the Sheikh's Harem (excerpt follows)

The next, and last, book in this series wasn't planned. But I had to know what happened to Ashley! And so *Taken for the Sheikh's Harem* was born. **A powerful sheikh, a feminist academic, and a harem...** An excerpt follows.

You can check out all my books on the following pages. And, if you'd like an email letting you know when my latest release has been published, you can sign up to my email list via my website—dianafraser.com.

Happy reading!

Diana

TAKEN FOR THE SHEIKH'S HAREM

BOOK 5 OF SHEIKHS OF HAVILAH

A powerful sheikh, a feminist academic, and a harem...

Dr. Ashley Maitland is an academic who is determined to leave her painful past behind her and forge a university career for herself—even if that means she has to write a sensational book about harems.

So she travels to the medieval country of Irem which is as mysterious as its king, Sheikh Zyir. But there she discovers that the only way she can complete her research is to join the sheikh's harem!

She knew where to go. There could be no doubting it. Rising above the city stood the ancient palace of Irem—commanding and dominating—home to the absolute ruler of this mysterious and unique country.

Excerpt

It seemed she was expected, and gates opened as she approached. She drove into the courtyard, which was central to the palace. She parked where shown and adjusted her scarf and abaya.

"This way, madam," a Bedouin manservant said, bowing.

"Thank you."

She swung her backpack onto her shoulder and followed him across the courtyard.

Suddenly she felt the tiny hairs on the back of her neck prickle and she looked up to her left. Someone moved behind the unglazed latticed windows. Then they were gone again. She shrugged. She guessed she'd have to get used to being observed—she was very much a stranger in a very foreign land.

Ashley followed the servant along a cloister-like corridor reminiscent of a medieval cathedral, with its stone-flagged floor and archways whose stone was carved into decoration, which had been muted by weather and touch, over the years. The very ground she walked on was dipped in the middle where people's feet had worn away the pale stone over thousands of years.

Despite its ancient origins, its design provided welcome relief from the scorching desert. In fact, the whole of the city seemed to be semi-underground, and cooler because of it. It was what it must have been like for many of the ancient civilizations, of which this was one of the few remnants. It was what made it unique. But she didn't have the opportunity to look at it now. She had a meeting with the official with whom she'd completed her bookings—Sheikh Riyz. Once she'd met with him, she'd been promised an audience with the king.

The servant opened the door, bowed, and stood aside for her to enter. She walked into the austere reception room, momentarily dazed by the sudden glitter of light on gold, of sunshine on topaz. Then she turned to see a tall, forbidding-looking man staring at her. He looked to be around thirty years of age and dressed in plain robes with no ornamentation, nothing to show he was of any consequence. Elaheh, who'd never met the present king, only his father, had told her not to expect anything as casual as her and Xander's own countries. And, as Ashley didn't consider there was anything casual about them, her imagination had failed her on how much more formal Irem would be. At least his administrative staff didn't appear to stand on ceremony.

Ashley walked over to him and extended her hand. His eyes hadn't shifted from her.

"You must be Sheikh Ryiz," she said, forcing a smile to hide her nerves. His impassive face didn't move an inch. It could have been carved from stone. "It's good to meet you."

The man accepted her hand, and it engulfed hers. "*As-salamu Alaykum*, Dr. Maitland. Welcome to my country."

"*Wa Alaykum as-salam.*" Ashley returned the traditional words of greeting. "Thank you, it's good to be here. I'm very *excited* to be here," she added, thinking some flattery might help her. "I've heard such tantalizing stories about your country."

He gave a small grunt as his eyes narrowed. "I trust you had a pleasant journey."

"It was amazing. I didn't expect to see such expansive fields of flowers."

"Ah, the results of the heavy rains we've had."

"It's brought the desert to life."

"Indeed. But it will also bring with it locusts—the scourge of plenty."

Sheikh Ryiz might have been approachable by email, but he sure was a pessimist. He looked pretty forbidding, too. Nothing like she'd imagined. She wanted to look around, to absorb more details of this impressive, but austere, room, but she couldn't take her eyes off him.

He gestured to an archway, through which she could see a courtyard. But, as soon as she followed him outside, she thought it could hardly be called a courtyard, because it was too luxuriously furnished. A low, cushioned seating area, decorated with jewel-like rugs and cushions, surrounded a small pond with a rill of rippling water. It was an exquisitely beautiful oasis.

"Please, take a seat. I'm sure you'd like some refreshments after your trip."

She was about to accept because she was both thirsty and hungry, but remembered her manners. "No, thank you, I don't wish to trouble you."

He smiled as if realizing what she was doing, but

nodded in appreciation. "I assure you, it is no trouble. It would be an honor to extend our hospitality to you."

She couldn't refuse the polite second offer. "Then, thank you, that would be very welcome. It's been a long ride."

As she took the offered seat, the doors swung open as if they'd received some hidden command, and two men entered the room, carrying a distinctive, crescent-beaked dallah, together with two small cups and a plate of dates. They arranged the dates and coffee, infused with fresh ground cardamon, on the table.

Ashley made herself comfortable, which wasn't hard. The place was designed for comfort, designed to seduce. The word popped into her head unbidden, and she stole a glance at the sheikh, whose gaze hadn't left hers. She racked her brain to think of something to say.

"The climate is very comfortable here, in the city. I thought it would be much hotter." She glanced at the elaborate air vent which brought whatever breeze flowed high across the desert skies, down into the courtyard room. Together with the semi-transparent shades slung overhead, filtering the sunlight, they cooled the temperature. "I've read about the windcatchers here, but I've never experienced one before."

"Of course. My country has been closed to visitors for too long."

She raised her eyes, interested. "Your king intends to make changes?"

"Yes."

She waited for him to elaborate. He didn't. Instead, he nodded to a woman who was waiting by the door. The woman kneeled before them and poured a small amount of coffee into each cup. She withdrew once more, her gaze downward, as if she were in prayer. Such subservience made Ashley feel uncomfortable.

She looked up at Sheikh Riyz and realized he hadn't taken his eyes off her. It made her feel even more uncomfortable. She'd thought he would take her to the king, but it looked as if he had the task of screening her first. She had to make sure she passed the test, whatever it was. She needed this man to approve of her before she moved onto the next stage.

"You look uncomfortable, Dr. Maitland."

She looked away, embarrassed and surprised that he'd been able to read her mind so easily. She took a sip of the hot coffee, known locally as *gahwa*, and set it back down again. She shrugged and looked up at him. "It's a new land, new ways. It'll take a little while to become accustomed to them."

He frowned. "I understood you were an expert in our ways. Is that not the case?"

"Well, I am in one sense. I mean I *know* them, I've studied them, but being here and experiencing them first hand is another thing entirely."

He nodded. "Yes, one can never know something unless one has lived it. I agree."

He had a low voice, quietly authoritative, and Ashley could see why the king might have chosen him as his advisor. His eyes echoed that authority—penetrating and unreadable. He held her gaze for a few moments, and she thought that that would be how it would feel to have her brain scanned by a computer. Except this man was no computer. He held the key to her future, and if she felt uncomfortable before, she felt something else now—she felt acutely feminine. His eyes seemed to move from investigating her to an appreciation shown by his warming gaze and a tug at his lips as a glimmer of a smile settled on them. She practically purred under that caressing look. Maybe a brief flirtation with the king's advisor wouldn't go amiss.

"Tell me," he said, leaning forward, his body now echoing both the gaze of his eyes and his velvety caress of a voice, "what is it you want, Dr. Ashley Maitland?"

His words brought her crashing back down to earth. A blush flooded her pale cheeks, and she looked around, searching for an escape. He might be seducing her with his eyes and voice, but he suspected her intent. Why leave it until now to ask that question? Breathe, Ashley told herself. Keep calm. He's just testing you. She summoned a smile from nowhere.

"What do I want? I want to see the king, sir. I seek his permission to carry out research in Irem."

He sat back, considering her. "And this research of yours..."

He hesitated and nerves made her jump in. "It's on—"

He held up his hand; it was all he needed to do to make her stop mid sentence.

"I know what your research is on, Dr. Maitland. What I don't know is what you intend to do with it."

She narrowed her eyes, trying to figure out what he wanted to know. Whatever it was, she'd give it to him. She was desperate. She hadn't come all this way for nothing. Her entire career depended on it. "Do with it?"

"I want to know what's in it for my country, Dr. Maitland. It's all very well allowing you access to privileged information, providing you with resources, but we need to know how this will benefit Irem."

"Oh!" She nodded, trying to figure out how she could re-shape her research to meet this new requirement. This man, and therefore presumably the king, had no interest in research for research's sake. They knew their buildings, and their world. To them, her research was of interest for something very different. But what? "I have no wish to do anything which might harm Irem." She hesitated. She had no idea if he wanted her to keep the research to themselves, or to spread it far and wide. But she had to come clean, because as soon as she left this country she'd be shouting her work from the rooftops. She drew in a deep breath. He was attentive, patient, waiting for her to speak.

"I intend to publish it," she said, the words tumbling out. "I have interest from an international publisher who is keen to publish the book as they believe it will have broad appeal. And I will write the book for that market— not as an academic text." She held her breath, hoping she wouldn't be turned around and expelled from the country. "It will have popular appeal," she added, for clarification.

He gave a small grunt and for the first time lifted his gaze from hers, and nodded his head. "That is satisfactory."

Relief fell off her like a burden. "Good," she smiled. "Ah, that's a relief. And, believe me, I know there's wide international interest in the subject."

For the first time, Sheikh Ryiz appeared surprised. "Is that correct?"

"Yes, indeed."

"Good. Then, Dr. Maitland, maybe we should begin with a quick tour of the city."

"Yes, that would be lovely, thank you."

He rose with the ease of someone who was accustomed to sitting cross-legged while Ashley tried her best to rise gracefully. She was glad of her early training in ballet—given up when the teacher had ruined her life forever at thirteen by telling her bluntly there was no way that someone of her height and curves would ever be a ballerina. So, although she was no slender waif, Ashley still knew how to move with grace.

While Sheikh Riyz exchanged a few words with the woman who, Ashley thought, bowed with unnecessary humility, she turned away, unwilling to watch a woman lower herself in such a way. As she did so, she caught sight of a couple of chrysalides, clinging to the underside of a butterfly tree.

She stroked the leave to which one clung. She turned suddenly, a sixth sense alerting her to his gaze.

"The *khof al gamal* flowers are extraordinary this year."

"So are the butterflies," she said. "There are a lot of chrysalides on this plant. I don't know about locusts, but it looks like the rains are also making the butterflies happy. And that has to be a good thing."

"Happy butterflies," he repeated, coming to a halt a few steps from her. He turned to face her. "I have to say that I have never considered whether a butterfly is happy. It simply goes about its business."

She shrugged and stroked the length of the chrysalis before pushing away the leaves to reveal yet more clusters. "Maybe, but who are we to say whether butterflies have feelings? Besides, the two things aren't exclusive." She looked at him. "Business and happiness, I mean."

He raised an eyebrow and his dark eyes held humor which she hadn't seen before. But he didn't speak.

She refused to be cowed by a glowering, silent man—no matter how compelling he was. "Surely your king would like to know that you're happy in your work?"

He shrugged. "Maybe you should ask him."

"I would if I could meet him. I mean, I understand that you're screening me for him, but I hope I can get to see the king soon." He still didn't speak. "I mean, it's good of him to take the time to meet with me, although I guess there's not a lot of distraction here in the middle of the desert." She smiled again, hoping to get a positive response.

The humor in the man's eyes disappeared.

"You'd be surprised, Dr. Maitland, how busy a ruler of a kingdom can be, even in the middle of a desert."

She realized her mistake. "Yes, I'm sure." She fell into step beside him. "Are we going to meet the king now?"

He didn't miss a step.

"You've met him already, Dr. Maitland."

∾

ABOUT THE AUTHOR

I write romances with stories which make you turn the pages, and characters who feel real—whether they be sheikhs, billionaires, knights or everyday people whose lives are usually far from everyday (at least in my books).

A little about me...I'm an avid people watcher, hopeless romantic and dreamer who spends far too much time gazing out the window, imagining scenes where people struggle with life and emotions but always end up happily. Because, yes, I'm also an eternal optimist!

I live in beautiful New Zealand, just north of Wellington in a small village by the sea. It's here, in a sunny window seat overlooking the hills and trees, that I write my books.

Wherever you are in the world, welcome to my little corner, creating worlds where people struggle with life and emotions but are always rewarded with love and happiness in the end. Because that's non negotiable!

I hope you enjoy my books.

Diana

ALSO BY DIANA FRASER

—British Billionaires—

The Billionaire's Contract Marriage

The Billionaire's Impossible CEO

The Billionaire's Secret Baby

British Billionaire Boxed Set (complete series)

—The Sheikhs' Convenient Brides—

Stranded with the Sheikh

Seduced by the Sheikh

—Diamond Sheikhs—

At the Sheikh's Command

At the Sheikh's Bidding

At the Sheikh's Pleasure

Diamond Sheikhs Boxed Set (complete series)

—Secrets of the Sheikhs—

The Sheikh's Revenge by Seduction

The Sheikh's Secret Love Child

The Sheikh's Marriage Trap

Secrets of the Sheikhs Boxed Set (complete series)

Awakening his Lady

Norfolk Knights Boxed Set (1-3)

Defending his Lady

Honoring his Lady